UNTIL MISTER

CUBS FOR RENT #5

CHARITY PARKERSON

--Warning: This book is intended for readers over the age of 18.

Copyright © 2020 Charity Parkerson
Editor: Hercules & Consultants
ISBN: 978-1-946099-62-4
All rights reserved.

Wren thrives on being wicked. Haven needs to steer clear of his brand of trouble. They are both just trying to survive.

Most people consider Wren as born blessed. He has the looks of an angel, the morals of a devil, and isn't afraid to use whichever trait he needs most for every situation. What his looks won't buy him, his connections will. As the son of a famous actor, there isn't a door in society blocked to him. Unfortunately, his father blew through his money long before dying of a drug overdose, leaving Wren to work to pay his way. It's a good thing he has a body men can't resist and a personality to match. The last thing he needs is a controlling ex BDSM master getting in his way.

Haven aka Mister is just trying to get through the day. Between his bestselling BDSM how-to books and his job at Cubs for Rent, he isn't hurting for money, but his personal life is a different story. It's dead in the water. After ruining his relationship with the only man Haven cares to love, he has no intention of ever dating again. He knows he's poisonous and he won't risk hurting anyone else. That's exactly why he has to stay away from Wren. Too bad he can't.

With an unexplainable draw pulling them closer together, it's only a matter of time before they break. But there's more to Wren than a pretty face, and he's in bigger danger of losing everything than even he knows. Unless Haven can save him, that is.

ONE

BEING HIRED to demo for Dex Wise, a billionaire known for creating reality TV shows that had rabid followings, was a bit intimidating. While his friend Orion had predicted Haven's BDSM demos would become a growing trend and make Haven rich, Haven didn't believe anyone at Cubs for Rent had been prepared for how in demand Haven would be. Since he did upwards of five demos a night on the weekends, he had gotten pretty good at transporting his gear from one job to the next. He had just spent an hour at Dex Wise's house, rubbing elbows with the stars. That was one place Haven never expected to be. Dex Wise was a billionaire TV genius. He was the man behind countless explosive reality shows. Haven had no idea why the guy had hired him.

Haven had spent his hour-long demonstration talking to a crowd of guests who pretended he wasn't there as they milled around chatting. It was uncomfortable but familiar. Haven was getting used to being invisible. He froze with one hand on the lid of his trunk and the other on his work bag. His mind drifted.

I wish you were dead. Those words were never far from Haven's thoughts. Haven swore they were still every bit as loud tonight as they had been when he first heard them three months ago. Every time his mind went there, he could see his ex, Kevin's, face. He could picture Kevin's hatred and feel the punch to his chest as if it had just happened. Haven couldn't fall over dead and give Kevin his wish, but he could and would kill his heart. He owed Kevin that much. Haven deserved to be alone for the rest of his life with his guilt. The more he sequestered himself from others, the less people noticed his presence. It was fucking odd. He wished he didn't still miss Kevin so much.

"You dropped this on the way out the door."

As the sultry words washed over Haven, he shook himself from the black hole trying to suck him under. He focused on the polished blond angel. The boy, who couldn't be more than twenty, held out one of Haven's crops. Haven pasted on a fake smile and reached for it.

"Thank you. I didn't even notice."

Light green eyes sparkled with life, good humor, and a certain level of naughtiness. "It's no problem. I was headed this way anyhow. As a policy, I always leave Dex's parties before the real perverts turn up, and I have another job to get to." Before Haven could inquire, the boy spoke over him. "You work for Cubs for Rent, right? Me too. I'm Wren."

Haven held out his hand for Wren to shake. "Charmed. I'm Haven."

Wren's eyebrow rose. Just the one. There was so much cockiness in the gesture that Haven fought a laugh. This one was trouble. "Haven? I thought your name was Mister."

"I go by both," Haven admitted. "I'm an author. Mister Haven is my pen name." He didn't bother explaining Mister was something subs called him. That was in his past.

"Where are you off to now?" Wren asked, moving past the name issue.

Haven checked his watch. "I believe my next job is in Rosedale. What about you?"

A spark of challenge entered Wren's eyes. "I'm a dancer at The Woodshed. I'd invite you to come see me, but I'm afraid you might spank me for being bad." He winked.

Despite Wren's over-the-top flirtatious personality, Haven couldn't stop smiling. "You don't have to worry. I don't spank people anymore."

"Shame."

A chuckle escaped Haven. "I don't hang out at places called The Woodshed either."

A mock gasp escaped Wren. "Scandal. Well, I guess I'll just go then before I taint you with my hussiness."

"Is that a word?"

"It is now," Wren said, taking a step backward.

Despite his best efforts, Haven couldn't stop his gaze from skimming Wren's body. He was breathtaking and trouble. Haven could smell that last bit from a mile away.

Wren's smile hitched up a notch. "I saw that."

"What?" Haven tried looking as innocent as possible.

"Mhmm," Wren hummed, not bothering to say what they both knew. Haven had been checking him out. He turned away but took one last parting shot over his shoulder. "No staring at my ass. You're above such things."

Haven bit his bottom lip to keep from laughing.

His smile refused to be controlled. He shook his head as he slipped behind the wheel of his car. With no input from his brain, Haven's gaze slid Wren's way again. Wow. His ass was perfect. Haven shook his head again. Probably from dancing all night. Hussiness was sexy.

Before Haven could start his car, he spotted Dex weaving his way through the parked cars lining the driveway. Curiosity got the best of him. The man seemed to be locked on Wren like a laser. As Haven looked on, Dex intercepted Wren at the door of a new Barracuda. Haven knew he should move along, but he also didn't want to start his car and give his eavesdropping away. Dex stood a little too close. Wren didn't push him away. Haven watched as Dex handed Wren what looked to be money. From where they stood, between two parked cars, Haven couldn't see much from his angle. He also couldn't hear the words exchanged, but Haven knew Wren was flirting by the way he sparkled. Just the idea made Haven smile.

Too late, Haven realized he shouldn't be watching. Dex disappeared—like he had dropped to his knees. Wren's back hit the passenger side door of the car. His expression turned winded as he tilted his chin up and sucked air. Haven's eyebrows creeped upward as he realized Dex was blowing Wren in the middle of the driveway. He tried looking away. It wasn't happening. The air thickened. His heart rate kicked up. Wren's chin dropped and their gazes met, making Haven realize Wren could see him every bit as clearly as Haven could see Wren. Haven knew he should look away. He couldn't leave without giving himself away to Dex, but he shouldn't be watching. The thing was, he was held completely hostage by Wren's stare. His face was flushed and looked two steps beyond turned on. Haven's fingers curled until his hands were fists—like he tried physically to hold on to his sanity. Wren's full lips parted on a pant. Haven's cock strained against the zipper of his jeans. He knew the exact moment Wren's orgasm hit. Haven sucked in a gasp, as if it had happened to him. Wren never broke eye contact even as he visibly fought to breathe.

Dex came to his feet and Haven tore his gaze away. He focused on his dashboard, seeing nothing but Wren's face in his head. Haven was hard-pressed to explain why the moment had been so hot. While it was true he hadn't had sex in ages, he had jerked off to hotter porn. There was something about Wren. Haven couldn't put his finger on it. All he knew was, he needed to steer clear from that exact brand of trouble. Against his will, his gaze slid back that direction. Wren was gone. So too was the bright red Barracuda. Fuck. His body craved release. He checked his watch. There was only twenty minutes left before he needed to be at his next job. Haven started his car. He had to leave this nonsense behind. Kevin had wished him dead, Haven reminded himself. He couldn't let himself want blond boys with wicked green eyes. That part of his life was over. His tensed muscles told a different story. He craved the surge of power that came with bending someone to his will, especially a wicked blond sprite with a naughty spirit. God help him. He could never, ever see Wren again.

ALL NIGHT, WREN PICTURED HAVEN'S FACE. A smile that felt wicked even to him kept tugging at his lips. The tips were bigger than usual. Wren had a feeling it was due to his mood. He loved a good blow job as much as the next guy, but there was something about Haven watching. Haven claimed he no longer spanked people, and he didn't visit clubs like this one. The plot thickened. He liked a good mystery. No matter Haven's claims, he hadn't looked away as

Wren had pumped Dex's mouth full of cum. A man who watched was a man who joined, and Wren loved quantity. That was obvious by the pile of money at his feet.

The cage where he currently danced kept him safe from hands but left plenty of space for bills to get shoved through the bars. The more he teased and skin he showed, the higher the money pile grew. Wren wasn't above getting dirty as hell to make bank. He had expensive taste. While spending time with Dex paid his way, Wren had learned to never put his eggs in only one basket. All it took was one wrong move with the right controlling man and he would be homeless. Fuck that. His real daddy had already died, leaving him penniless and at the mercy of others. Wren had no intention of ever going down that road again. As long as he kept his looks and didn't grow morals or fall into feelings, he would be fine. A normal life was for the weak. While this place didn't pay anywhere near what dating did, he had too many responsibilities to be at anyone's mercy.

"I'm told you're Sparrow here."

Wren glanced down at the yelled words. Haven stood below him, staring up at him with his hands shoved in his pockets and a small smile hovering on his lips. While holding the bars, Wren dropped to his haunches and held the man's stare. He was dangerously sexy with his dark blond curly hair and glasses. "Look who decided to crawl through the mud with the rest of us. You're not the only man with two names. I can't use my real one here and have people following me home." He paused for effect. "But you know who I am. Did you come just to see me?"

Haven cast a look around the club filled with caged dancers and stage entertainment before focusing on Wren once more. "It would seem so, since I'm still not interested in a place called The Woodshed."

Wren tossed his head back and roared with laughter. For some strange reason, he loved that Haven pretended to be above visiting a strip club. Yet he was here. For Wren. An odd spurt of joy and butterflies fluttered in Wren's stomach. There was something about this one.

Wren swiped at his eyes. "Hang out for ten more minutes and I'll be free."

Haven looked like a runner, but he nodded. "I'll be right here."

Yes, he would. Wren intended to keep him too entertained to get away. With a wink, Wren went back to dancing. He kept time with the music. His body moved while his gaze never wavered from the man below him. He was turned on by the heated way Haven watched him and completely incapable of hiding it in his current state of undress. Without an ounce of shame, Wren admitted he was used to getting his way. He liked attention from men of his choosing. Wren wanted Haven. Unabashedly kinky men who were also hot were rarer than most people thought. As he held Haven's stare, Wren embraced the truth. He wouldn't stop until he had this one, and he wasn't above using every trick in his arsenal.

HAVEN HAD NO FUCKING CLUE WHAT HE WAS doing here. He was pretty sure he was losing his mind. No matter how hard he fought himself, Haven hadn't stopped thinking about Wren since driving away from Dex Wise's house. While that was a red flag, screaming he should stay away, Haven also needed to know more. Something in his gut brought him here. As he had watched Wren's perfect body, moving in time with the music, he had a bad feeling it was another part of his anatomy, lower than his gut, that brought him back to Wren. Goddamn. Wren was mesmerizing. Haven could practically feel the naughtiness vibrating from him when he danced. He would be shameless in his kinks.

Haven hadn't been this tempted in a long time. He couldn't lie to himself. That was the real reason he was leaned against the driver's side door of Wren's car, waiting where security had directed him until Wren finished changing. It made sense they had a way of sneaking the men out, so they wouldn't get mobbed. Haven fought for anything at all to think about other than Wren's body. Wren had been visibly aroused while dancing for Haven. It wasn't like he could hide it in a tiny, almost nonexistent thong. Haven's body burned. He drew a slow breath in through his nose. Getting turned on was pointless. He couldn't act on it. That part of his life was over. One man dead and another with a permanent heart condition was enough marks against his soul. He wasn't meant to be loved.

The side door of the building opened, and a security guard looked out before escorting Wren outside. With a quiet word from Wren, the man disappeared back inside, and Wren headed his way. In light jeans and a dark shirt, Wren shouldn't still stand out. He did. Haven fought a wave of possessiveness that terrified him. Nothing good ever came from that place inside him.

"Hey."

Wren winked. "Hey, gorgeous. I'll admit I'm surprised you waited. You looked like a runner for sure."

Haven couldn't stop smiling. "Why would I run?"

Wren shrugged. "You tell me. Why don't you spank people any longer? What's your story?"

No way that conversation was happening. "Maybe I could take you for a drink instead."

"I don't drink and I'm only twenty."

Damn. Of course, he was. "I didn't say it had to be alcoholic. Unless you're telling me you're an alien who doesn't need hydration."

A musical-sounding laugh burst from Wren. It hit Haven in the chest. "There's a twenty-four-hour diner down the street. We could walk."

"I would like that," Haven said, offering his arm.

As Wren slipped his hand into the crook of Haven's elbow and steered him toward the diner, Haven silently lectured himself. He was making a friend. Haven wasn't looking to start anything romantic or sexual. They both worked for Cubs for Rent. That gave them common ground. He had pretty thoroughly fucked any chance of getting close to Toby, Loyal, Orion, Tucker, or Jericho by losing his shit when he learned Toby had kissed his ex, Kevin. Even though he didn't plan to date again, Haven also didn't want to be completely alone in the world. Wren seemed nice and they already knew each other's dirt... for the most part. There would be no misunderstandings. Just friendship.

"So, tell me, Mister Haven, was this your first trip to a strip joint or your first trip back after trying to fly right?"

"My first trip ever," Haven admitted.

Wren stopped at the restaurant door and cast Haven a disbelieving look. "How has a BDSM master never been to a nudie bar?"

Haven shrugged. It was hard not to get lost in Wren's eyes. They were beautiful. There was something familiar about them. "I don't hang out in any clubs any longer, but when I did, I only went to fetish places." A smirk pulled at his lips. "I've always found men crawling to be so much hotter than men dancing, no offense."

With a chuckle, Wren held open the door for Haven. "None taken. I'm not for everyone."

Haven paused with one foot inside the diner. His gaze moved Wren's way. He held Wren's stare, letting his hunger show. "Don't put words in my mouth. I didn't say that. You know damn well you're wanted by everyone."

A bark of laughter escaped Wren. He covered his mouth, obviously trying to smother the sound. Haven's smile grew. He was glad he had stepped out of his own head and shown up. Time with Wren felt a lot like exactly what he needed.

Wren waited until they were seated and looking at the menu before striking again. "So, tell me, how does a man who doesn't believe in spanking anymore end up teaching other people how to do it?"

Haven stared harder at his menu to buy himself time. He was never sure how much of himself he should show others. In the end, he knew he had to be honest with Wren. He couldn't let Wren think this was anything more than Haven trying to be friends. He no longer had a heart to share with anyone.

He set his menu aside. "It's not that I don't believe in what I teach. In the right hands and in a trusting relationship, lifestyle living can be a beautiful thing. The sexual health of a relationship colors the entire bond. If people think sex doesn't matter when two people are in love, they've never had a shitty sex life. The thing is, it's not right in my hands. I can't be trusted to treat someone as a treasure rather than a possession. Everyone who has ever given me their heart and submission has regretted it. I've done a lot of unforgivable things. So I don't do those things anymore."

Wren cocked his head to one side, looking intrigued. "What things don't you do? BDSM, dating, or sex in general?"

"All of the above."

"Unfortunate," Wren said, pulling an adorable disgruntled face.

No matter the topic, it was impossible not to smile in Wren's presence. Haven wanted to know him. "What about you? Are you dating Dex for real? Or did I witness something semi-illegal earlier?"

Wren snorted. He didn't have an ounce of shame and Haven loved it. "I was officially off the clock, and no. We're not dating. Dex is Dex. He's a billionaire with an endless supply of men who are trying to break into acting. Someone like him will never, ever be exclusive with anyone. And before you ask, no. I'm not interested in being tied down by him either. I just... know him, and his kinks, so he knows he can turn to me. That's it. I guess we're friends... in as much as Dex is capable of caring about anyone." Wren's bright smile returned. "Not that I saw you complaining earlier."

Haven smirked. It was out of his control. Some

things were ingrained in his personality too deeply. "I doubt anyone has ever turned down an invitation —silent or otherwise—to watch you come."

Before Wren could respond, a waitress appeared. They both ordered tea before going back to staring at each other. Wren spoke and Haven listened. He swore he understood every word and answered in kind, but nothing stuck. Haven was too enthralled. Wren screamed untainted happiness. Haven wanted to soak up every ounce and hold it to his chest. He wondered if he had ever been like Wren. Even though Haven was only twenty-seven, he didn't remember ever being young. He had always been too much. Felt things too deeply. He was so confident that it circled back around to insecure. Haven was so intense that his love felt like hate.

It wasn't until they were walking side by side, elbows brushing, that the cool night air brought Haven back to reality. They could only be friends. Wren's light didn't belong to him and he would snuff it out anyhow. Still, he had enjoyed himself more than he had in a long damn time.

"You're pretty amazing," Haven said, apropos to nothing and in the middle of Wren talking about something entirely different. They were almost to Wren's car. He couldn't let the man get away without saying something. "I understand why Dex keeps coming back to you. Sorry. I had to say that before you made it to your car. I imagine we both have too hectic of schedules to run into each other again."

A sweet smile touched Wren's lips. It was at such odds with his usual wicked one that Haven couldn't look away. "I don't know. I have a feeling we'll cross paths again. Thank you for the drink and chat. It was nice."

"I would say anytime, but I'm sure I can't afford you."

Wren snorted. "Later, Mister," Wren said, turning away.

"It's Haven."

Wren waved over his shoulder like he didn't care. Haven couldn't stop smiling. "By the way," Wren said, turning back his way before he made it to his car. "About what you said earlier, I don't think anyone is completely unforgivable. One of these days, I think you'll be back to demanding someone to get on their knees."

A flash of irrational anger hit Haven at the claim. Wren was so sparkly and obviously untouched by reality. He had no idea what real pain looked like. He didn't know what it felt like to kill the thing he loved. To watch it die. "What a charmed life you must've lived if you think nothing is unforgivable."

In a flash, Wren's eyes went dead. His boyish smile fell, leaving Haven staring at a stranger. "There's never been a damned thing about my life that's charmed. How nice it must be to use your past mistakes as a shield to shut everyone out, while the rest of us are forced to fake it so we don't starve. Excuse me while I wipe away a tear for you. I have to get home." He turned away.

Guilt overwhelmed Haven. It hit him why Wren's light green eyes looked so familiar. They looked just like Sawyer's eyes—he had killed that boy too. "Wren." Haven waited until Wren looked his way, walking backward toward his car, to apologize. "I wasn't trying to hurt you."

The bright smile that Wren always wore came back. He had visibly rescinded Haven's invitation to see the real him. "Yes you were. That's who you are, baby. You're a man who revels in other people's pain. I'd tell you to monetize that, but I guess you already have. Have a nice life, Mister Haven." Wren turned away and jumped behind the wheel of his car, taking his over-the-top happiness and inner light with him, and leaving Haven cold. If nothing else, Haven was consistent. He always ensured no one wanted anything else to do with him. Damn.

WREN STARED AT HIS BEDROOM CEILING AND chewed the side of his thumbnail. He should be exhausted, but he wasn't. His mind raced, as usual. He had always been cursed with too much energy. His body refused to rest. No matter how hard he tried, Wren's mind kept circling back to Haven. While the guy was hot with his dark blonde curly hair and dark blue eyes that sparkled with intelligence, that wasn't why Wren couldn't stop thinking about him. Haven was unhappy. People confused Wren. He knew so many men who had it all with zero real responsibilities on their plate, and still, they were miserable. Wren didn't understand. He wanted to be bitter about it, but really, he was just confused. Wren wanted to understand, but he couldn't.

His phone buzzed, drawing his gaze to the clock. It was almost five in the morning. Before long, the sun would be up, and so would he with no sleep again. He snagged the cord of his phone and dragged the device closer until he could grab it. After unplugging it, Wren tossed the cord aside and checked the message.

Dex: *I finally got everyone out of here. If you're not asleep, you should come back. I'd make it worth your while.*

Wren set the phone aside without responding. He would text Dex back later and claim he had been sleeping. A wave of weariness washed over him at the thought of going back to Dex's house. An unexpected smile tugged at his lips. Haven had asked if they were dating. That was funny. People like Dex didn't date. Hell, people like Wren didn't either. No one took a real look at Wren's life and was suddenly overwhelmed with the desire to be a permanent part of it. Wren didn't have the option to quit dating for pay or stripping to make what dating didn't cover. No one wanted someone like him. Not really.

For a minute, though, Haven had watched Wren like he wanted him. Wren couldn't recall anyone looking at him the way Haven had—hungry, except darker. For a second, in that cage, Wren had been grateful for the bars keeping him safe. Haven had watched him like he would do things to Wren that would hurt. His heated expression flashed through Wren's mind. A loud pant escaped Wren. His eyes fell closed. Haven was waiting inside his head. Wren could picture Haven's teeth sinking into his skin. His cock strained against the band of his underwear, trying to climb out. Wren slipped his hand inside and palmed his erection. He doubted Haven would ever get on his knees for anyone, but Wren had been watching him from above earlier. Haven had beautiful lips. Wren wondered how they tasted. For half a second, he had hoped Haven would kiss him earlier, but Haven had made no attempt to touch Wren at all.

Wren liked being touched. Petted. Probed. He liked everything. Damn. He really wanted Haven to fuck him—hard. His body burned. Wren tossed back the covers. Fuck it. He would go see Dex. Haven didn't want him. In fact, Haven thought he was nothing but fluff. He snatched up his phone.

Wren: *I'll be there in ten.*

Dex: *Bring your toys.*

Wren didn't need Haven. Dex would make him forget. One man was as good as the next. None of them wanted him for real anyhow. He may as well get his share.

TWO

WHILE STANDING in Toby's kitchen, Haven debated with himself as Toby printed out his demo schedule and directions. He could get them emailed but coming over always gave Haven an excuse to stare at four different walls. The Kodiak brood had no reason to mess with Haven beyond business. Not since he had fucked up their friendship anyhow. Still, he didn't have anyone else to talk to and he liked them, even if they were done with him.

"You know Wren, right?" Haven tried to sound nonchalant. "We met last night, and he said he works for you too."

Toby kept his gaze locked on his laptop as he nodded. "Wren Carmichael. He's a smart cookie. I swear his rates are like ten times what everyone else charges, but no one complains, because he's so damn hard to book. Dex Wise always has him reserved, and if he actually has an open date on his calendar, it goes for major bank. It's insane."

Haven could see it. Wren was worth the money. Haven would pay a lot to have him... if Haven had been whole, that is. "What's his story?"

At his question, Toby's gaze slid from the laptop and locked on Haven. Haven had a bad feeling he had tipped his hand. He tried hard to keep his expression blank. Obviously finding nothing untoward in Haven's inquiry, Toby went back to focusing on work. He shrugged. "There's not much to tell to my knowledge. He's a hard worker. Never skips out on an appointment, which—as it turns out—happens a lot more than you'd think considering how much these guys are paid. Oh, he had a famous dad who died young."

"Are we talking about Wren?" Loyal asked, wheeling into the kitchen and obviously catching the tail end of Toby's speech. "I like him."

Tucker was right behind him. "Wren is awesome, but he's had a super hard life."

Haven fought the urge to dance in place. Tucker was exactly the kind of guy he needed. A gossip. "What do you mean?"

Tucker's chest swelled, obviously gearing up to tell the tale. He was amazing at being the center of attention. "Well, he started dating for pay at sixteen. Only exclusive clients and on the down low, of course, but he didn't have any other choice. His dad died of a drug overdose, leaving his little brother and him homeless."

"Oh yeah," Loyal said, snapping his fingers. "He was telling me about his brother. Finch, I think is his name. He's in a wheelchair too."

Tucker nodded. "He has cerebral palsy and needs twenty-four-hour care. Wren spends a lot of time at the nursing home where he lives. His care costs a fortune, and since his dad left them alone and broke, Wren has to do what he has to do."

Goddamn. Haven had accused him of having a charmed life. That pretty much summed up Haven's life, though. He fucked up everything he touched.

"Finch and Wren," Toby repeated, sounding absent. "Wonder who had the bird obsession?"

Tucker chuckled. "I believe it was some sort of tradition on their mom's side to have bird names. Her name was something similar too. Started with an s, I think."

"Sparrow."

At Haven's suggestion, Tucker perked up. "Yeah.

That's it. I believe she was some sort of dancer or something. She died after having Finch. I don't know. It was some complication that also caused Finch's issues."

"That's sad," Loyal said, mimicking Haven's thoughts. "We should hang out with that guy more often. Show our support. It sucks to handle everything alone when you have a lot going on."

Toby stared at his husband with pride etching his features. Haven understood why. Loyal was a good person. "We'll figure something out, angel." His gaze swung Haven's way. "Your schedule should be printing in my office. I'll go grab it."

Haven nodded and stared at his feet. Despite everyone's input on Wren, he didn't feel welcome here. Things were different now. Loyal's father was with Kevin and that made Haven the odd man out. As always, he fit nowhere, just as it had been his entire life, except when he had first met Kevin. That was the only time in Haven's whole life he had felt like he counted in the world. He was awesome at faking confidence. Life just fit him like trying to stretch a twin sized fitted sheet across a king-sized bed. It was hard and pointless work.

"Are you ready to get your ass kicked in basketball tomorrow? We're having a family day."

At Loyal's question, Haven's eyebrows rose. If Loyal wasn't looking at him, he would be certain the invite was for someone else. He shifted from one foot to the other in his discomfort. "Um. I'm sure you'd rather have your dad here than me."

Tucker and Loyal exchanged a glance. Tucker spoke first. "Well, I mean, he's still in California at that Vineyard resort."

"Oh." He wasn't sure why they thought he would know that. "That sounds nice. I'm glad he's getting a vacation."

Loyal and Tucker stared at him with matching closed expressions. "Oh," they said simultaneously.

Before he could ask, Toby reappeared with his schedule. He held it out to Haven. "I was thinking. You should come by tomorrow. We're having a cookout and whatnot. Maybe we could invite Wren too. I mean, we're completely wheelchair friendly here. Maybe he could bring his brother. With Jericho on his honeymoon, I don't think there'll be any hurt feelings. I mean, eventually, everyone will have to learn to get along anyhow. Kevin is family now."

Haven's brain completely short circuited, leaving him incapable of responding. Tucker and Loyal looked horrified while Toby looked like everything he said was the height of reason.

Toby's gaze moved from Haven to Loyal and back again. His expression underwent a series of changes that might have been comical under any other circumstances. "Shit. You didn't know."

Haven stiffened his spine and took a steadying breath. He had demanded Jericho love Kevin the way he deserved because Kevin would no longer allow Haven to love him. Jericho hadn't let Haven down. Funny how the pains in his chest didn't care about any of that. Haven cleared his throat. Even to his ears, it sounded painful. "What time do I need to be here tomorrow?" He would move on with his life without Kevin, even if it fucking killed him. Haven had been slogging through hell for over two years now without the other half of his heart. He assumed he wouldn't die from this. Maybe. Not that it mattered. He really had nothing left to live for anyhow.

FINCH WAS EXCITED TO MEET WREN'S FRIENDS. Wren didn't have the heart to tell his brother he didn't really have friends. He wasn't sure why Loyal had invited them over. He was grateful for Finch's sake. Finch rarely got to go anywhere other than short trips to the park. Technically, Wren didn't have custody of Finch yet. He only had visitation. Wren always felt like the shittiest brother on the planet. The guilt was thick. The least he could do was accept Loyal's invite for Finch's sake.

When Wren picked him up, Finch was dressed in his best. The nurses had warned Wren that Finch had gone all out. He wore a plaid dress shirt with a bow tie and suspenders. His blond hair was slicked back, and excitement flashed in Finch's green eyes. Wren beamed at the sight of him.

"Look at you, ladies' man. It's a good thing there won't be any girls at this thing. I'd have to beat them off with a stick."

Finch's huge lopsided grin made Wren's day. "My girlfriend wouldn't like it if girls were there."

Wren had a feeling Finch's girlfriend didn't know she was his girlfriend, but Finch was only twelve. It didn't matter. "Are you ready to get out of here? All the guys are really excited to meet you."

Finch made a valiant attempt to nod.

Wren couldn't take it. He stole his chance to hug him. "Dang, sweetie. I missed you yesterday."

"You have to work sometimes. It's okay. Love my brother. He's the best brother."

Wren's eyes burned. He wasn't, but he loved

Finch. As long as there was life in his chest, Finch would know he was loved, and Wren would always make sure he had the best of everything.

"Okay. Mushiness over, I swear. Your chariot awaits." Wren led the way. It was easier for Finch if he maneuvered his electric power chair. Plus, he deserved to hang on to what little independence he had. Wren did what he could by making sure Finch had a clear path and lowering the ramp on the van. He strapped the chair in place once Finch was inside. Wren didn't drive the specialized van very often. Only on their weekly trips to the park, or specialist visits. He didn't mind the extra work, though. If he could keep Finch with him all the time, he would. The truth was just hard sometimes. While Wren might feel better with Finch around, Finch was better off in the hands of professionals until Wren learned how to care for him in every aspect. Love was like that. It meant letting go when it was for the best. That didn't make living without Finch any easier.

In a show of nerves, Finch didn't make a sound the whole way there. Even as Wren unstrapped his chair, Finch stayed stubbornly mute. Normally, Finch never stopped talking. He always recapped every second Wren missed between visits. Not today. Today, he had turned to stone. Then Loyal appeared as Finch steered his chair off the van's lift. It was obvious he hadn't expected to find someone else in a chair like him. While their circumstances weren't the same, Finch wasn't the odd man out. That mattered.

Wren walked beside Finch, keeping pace with him so he didn't feel left behind as he tossed a wave toward Loyal. "Hey, Loyal. Thanks for the invitation." He motioned Finch's way. "This is my brother, Finch. Finch, this is Loyal."

"Hey, Finch." Loyal wheeled closer and held out his hand. "It's good to meet you. Wren is always telling me all about you. It's about time we convinced him to finally let us meet you." To Wren's relief, Loyal was extremely patient while Finch tried his best to shake hands. His muscle control wasn't the best, but Finch worked hard.

"It is nice to meet you too." Finch had a breathy voice that wasn't always easy to understand, but Loyal didn't act like he noticed.

"Wren was telling me some of your favorite games and I realized you have a lot in common with everyone here. Would you like to come hang out with us?"

Like that, it was on. Finch started talking,

making known not only his favorite games but every game he had ever played. Wren followed the pair to the backyard, breathing a sigh of relief. While he hadn't thought anyone would do anything to hurt Finch, he had worried Finch would feel out of place and withdraw. It seemed Finch had already made one friend. Wren would take it as a win.

As they rounded the corner, Wren's gaze landed on Haven. It was like he couldn't see anything else. His eyes had latched on to the man as if they were connected by an invisible lure. Damn. Haven really was gorgeous. His clothes were a little baggy and his hair was windblown. Still, Wren had to force himself to look away. While Loyal made the introductions, Wren made himself smile and nod at everyone, but his fucking eyeballs itched to slide Haven's way. Taken or not, there was plenty of eye candy there. Haven was hardly the only sexy guy within sight. Toby owned a business centered around hot men, and everyone there looked the part. Wren forced himself to keep his distance. He stayed glued to Finch's side. Wren had shown up today for his brother. Not only did Haven not matter at all, the guy had already proven he didn't think much of Wren. That last part helped Wren stay away.

WATCHING WREN AS HE KEPT HIS DISTANCE AND doted on his brother gave Haven... feelings. If Wren looked his way, even once after realizing Haven was there, Haven never caught him at it. Since he couldn't tear his gaze away from Wren, Haven had to accept Wren was ignoring him. Haven made it through the entire day without breaking, until dessert rolled around. Wren looked exhausted. With one elbow leaned on the arm of Finch's wheelchair, Wren played with Finch's hair while they talked in quiet tones. No one could question Wren's love. It was written in his every gesture. Haven grabbed two plates of apple pie and headed Wren's way. Wren held Haven's stare as he came to stand over them.

"Someone told me apple pie is your favorite." Haven prayed Wren would accept his olive branch.

"It's not my favorite, but it's Finch's." Wren's gaze slid Finch's way. "What do you say? Do you want some pie?"

Finch looked half asleep. He said something Haven couldn't understand, but Wren seemed to hear him just fine.

"That's fine, sweetie. We'll take it back with you. You can have it after you get some rest." Wren's features looked pinched. Haven's heart squeezed. While he was pretty sure he always came out as an ass, he hated that he had been so wrong about Wren. Haven had liked the idea of Wren being carefree, shameless, and untouched by life. Someone so beautiful should be like that. No one knew how tired he was of always being wrong. Just once, it would be nice to be the good guy.

"I'll get this wrapped up for you and I'll help you get this one home. I think the guys wore him out."

Wren shook his head. "It's okay. I can handle it."

Against his will, Haven's voice hardened. "I'll get this wrapped up and help you get him home." Haven couldn't help it. He was domineering and controlling by nature. It was in his DNA or something. He didn't know how to be someone else.

Wren nodded, letting him have his way. He went back to stroking Finch's hair and living inside himself. Haven wanted the shameless flirt back with something akin to desperation. He didn't understand why life had to be so damn hard all the time.

His black thoughts carried him through gathering leftovers for Finch and everyone passing around their goodbyes. The Kodiak family were all good people. Haven swore he wouldn't forget again. As Wren strapped in Finch's wheelchair, Haven swore he would try harder to be a good person too. Wren looked like he needed a few more unselfish people in his life.

"Give me the keys. I'll drive."

"Thanks, but I'm good." Wren looked ready to fall out.

Haven wasn't backing down. "Wren. I don't think you're weak. Now give me the goddamn keys and get in the goddamn van."

Wren passed the keys Haven's way. "Don't use that language in front of Finch." Without a backward look, Wren climbed into the passenger seat. Haven bit back a smile. Finch was sound asleep. Haven would take care of them.

Following Wren's directions, Haven easily found the home where Finch lived. After helping Finch out of the van, Haven climbed back behind the wheel and waited. Wren was all smiles as he headed inside with Finch, but there was a brittle edge to Wren—like he might crack any second. Fifteen minutes passed before Wren reappeared. Haven was fine to wait as long as needed. Wren made the trek back to the van with his head down. His shoulders looked heavy. Haven's heart ached. He swore he could feel the despondency rolling off Wren in waves. As he climbed into the passenger seat, Haven noticed his eyes and nose were red. He didn't look Haven's way. With his chin resting on his fist, Wren stared out the passenger side window. Haven waited. If Wren was going to fall apart, Haven didn't want to be driving when it happened.

"Stop looking at me like you know me. You don't know me."

Haven didn't respond. He didn't believe for a second Wren was really angry with him.

Wren covered his face and took a deep breath. When he dropped his hands, he stared straight ahead, looking lost. "He has friends here and they take good care of him."

Haven had a feeling Wren was talking to himself. Still, he went along. "He seems very happy."

Wren nodded. "He needs twenty-four-hour care. Even if I could do that alone, the court won't give me full custody. It's okay. He loves the nurses here."

Wren was definitely trying to convince himself. "I'm sure you visit all the time. You two seem very close." Wren swiped at his eyes. Fuck. He looked like his heart was ripping from his chest and Haven didn't know what to do. "I'm completely cool to hang out if you're not ready to leave him just yet. Don't worry over me at all."

Wren shook his head and swiped at his eyes

again. "I put him in bed. He needs to rest. It was a big day for him." Wren blew out a breath—like trying to force the hurt from his chest. "It's just really hard."

Haven got it. Real love meant doing what was right, even if the right thing hurt. If Finch needed around-the-clock medical care, it was possible he was better off here. Wren had to work sometimes. That didn't mean much to Wren's heart though, Haven imagined. Letting go was hard as hell when the heart screamed to hang on.

"Just drive," Wren said finally. "If you don't care, we can drop this off at my house and pick up my car. Sundays are my only day off."

"Jesus." Haven started the van. "You work for yourself. You should cut yourself some slack. Do you even sleep?"

Wren's gaze never wavered from the windshield. His voice still sounded dead. "Not really, no."

"What'll happen to Finch if you drop dead?"

"The state would completely take over his care." Wren said the words so calmly, as if it truly mattered not at all to him if he keeled over tomorrow, officially working himself to death.

Haven felt his temper rise. "I doubt Finch's feelings could give a damn about the state's care. You're his brother. He needs you alive."

Wren didn't respond. Haven chanced a quick glance his way. His eyes were still locked on the road and his arms were crossed over his chest—like he barely held himself together. Haven let it go. He recognized it wasn't his fight. Haven just felt helpless in the face of so much. He couldn't fathom how Wren felt.

"Tell me how to get to your house."

Wren dug out his phone, typed in the address, and set the phone in the cup holder, leaving Haven to follow the GPS suggestions while he leaned his head back and closed his eyes. Haven suppressed a sigh. He didn't know how to help. In truth, he didn't know how to do anything. All of Haven's life, he had pretty much been useless. Dealing with Wren was no different.

THREE

TO THE BOTTOM of his soul, Wren hurt. It was always this way when he left Finch. He already knew this would pour out in the unhealthiest way. That was okay. He didn't have to please anyone but himself. That was the upside of being permanently single. He could be as selfish and self-destructive as he liked. His gaze slid Haven's way. A muscle flexed in his jaw—like he ground his back teeth. Wren wondered what words he bit back. He had gotten kind of bossy with Wren today. It was hot. No matter how hard Haven tried beating down his domineering side, he couldn't escape his nature. No one could.

Haven pulled into Wren's driveway and looked his way. "Where do you want me to park this?"

Wren leaned his way, invading Haven's space.

Haven didn't try to get away as Wren hit the button on his keys to open the garage. Their faces were inches away. Wren purposely did his best to tempt Haven before he moved away. Haven tore his gaze away from Wren and focused on parking the van next to Wren's Barracuda. Wren never looked away. He invaded Haven's space again to hit the button, closing the door.

"Won't you have to just open it again for us to leave?"

Wren released a soft chuckle. Even to him, it sounded evil. He killed the van and palmed the keys before Haven could. He wanted the man at his mercy. "Let's go fuck instead."

Haven's head snapped around at Wren's suggestion—like there was no way he heard Wren right. "I'm sorry. What?"

After opening his door, Wren tilted his head toward the house. "You heard me. Let's go fuck."

Like he was frozen to his seat, Haven didn't budge. "Um. I'm not sure you're really in the right headspace—"

A burst of laughter exploded from Wren. "You're adorable. I didn't ask you to marry me. Hell, I didn't even suggest you be my man. Sex. In the house. Now. No strings." Wren slid from the van, refusing to entertain any further argument from Haven. Men didn't turn down sex. They were wasting time while Haven pretended to not be interested. As Wren shoved his keys in the door, Haven overcame him. His chest collided with Wren's back. Haven's lips brushed his nape before Wren found his head pulled back and Haven's mouth covered his. Wren's thoughts scattered. Haven's kiss was overwhelming. Haven was rough and in charge. Wren couldn't move. Haven was completely in control. He bit Wren's bottom lip hard enough to draw a gasp from Wren. Haven spun Wren in his arms and shoved Wren's body against the door. He was on fire. His cock leaked in his jeans. Wren had never been so aroused so quickly. Haven would be amazing. He wouldn't leave Wren unsatisfied. Haven's fingers dug into Wren's jaw as he pulled away. He held Wren in place, forcing Wren to hold his stare. "You're hurting. I don't take advantage of people. You know damn well you're wanted, but my soul is black enough without this mark against it."

Haven couldn't walk away from this. He was right. Wren was hurting. His heart needed a bandage. "You're not taking advantage of me. I'm using you."

For a moment, Haven simply stared at Wren expressionlessly. Then he slowly leaned in and touched his lips to Wren's. Wren's heart unexpectedly skipped a beat. Haven brushed the lightest kiss across Wren's lips. "Don't make me regret you." The quiet whisper barely caressed Wren's ears. "I already have enough shit I can't live with."

Wren took Haven's hand and headed inside. He tossed his keys on the kitchen counter as they passed. Wren didn't stop moving until he led Haven inside his bedroom.

"This is a nice house."

"Thank you," Wren said, toeing off his shoes.

Haven drew Wren back against his chest. His fingers encircled Wren's throat, gently holding him in place while silently reminding Wren who he had invited to bed. Wren's heart beat a little faster. Haven was a BDSM master. He might demand anything. The anticipation was real. Haven's other hand slid down Wren's body until he was tugging at the button of Wren's pants. His lips brushed the shell of Wren's ear. Haven suddenly stepped away, leaving Wren bereft.

"You're supposed to be in charge." He kicked out of his shoes and peeled off his shirt, giving Wren's eyes a treat. Haven crawled onto Wren's bed and settled onto his back before linking his fingers behind his head, as if waiting for Wren's next move. "You said you were using me. Use me."

Haven's chest and arms were sexy as hell. Wren worked in a strip club. He saw beautiful men unclothed all the time. This was different. Haven wasn't some young, pretty boy. He was slightly hairy with a solid chest that made Wren want to use it as a pillow. His mouth watered as he crossed the room. Haven watched him, looking curious and aroused. He was right to wonder what Wren would do next. Even Wren didn't know. Wren pulled his shirt up and over his head before tossing it aside. When he reached Haven's side, he bent and kissed Haven's stomach as he slid his zipper down. Wren pushed his pants down his hips as he moved lower and circled Haven's navel with his tongue.

"So sexy," Wren whispered against his stomach before going to work on Haven's jeans. "I want the whole picture." Despite Haven's demand that Wren be in charge, he still lifted his hips, helping as Wren undressed him. Once he was completely on display, Wren took his time, inspecting Haven's body. If he was uncomfortable with Wren eyeing his goods, Haven didn't show it. He stayed still, letting Wren play. Wren traced the thick vein in Haven's erection. Haven had a nice cock. Wren wanted to ride it.

"I hope you don't expect foreplay," Wren said, moving to the bedside table. He dug out a condom and lube.

"This isn't about me." Haven sounded calm and uncaring. Just the way Wren needed him.

"You're right. It's not." Even to Wren's ears, he sounded absent as he ripped into the wrapper. He rolled the sheath down Haven's erection. Wren couldn't think about Haven having feelings. He would never be free to love anyone, and he damn sure couldn't trust anyone to care about him. Once Haven's cock was covered and coated in lube, Wren held Haven's stare as he took off his underwear. Haven looked hungry—like his patience wore thin. A smile that felt evil even to him tugged at Wren's lips as he crawled onto the bed. He straddled Haven's body and stared down into the man's dark blue eyes.

"I like you," Wren admitted. He could give that much. "You look so adorable in your glasses. Do you want me to take them off?"

Haven shook his head. "I don't want to miss anything."

Wren still didn't move to do anything more than sit on Haven's stomach with his weight braced on his knees. He liked that Haven didn't make him do anything. It was nice having all the control, moving at his pace. "Did you expect me to be exciting? The wicked stripper who uses men to feel better?"

Haven's blank expression never cracked even as his hands slid up Wren's thighs. "What I think about you would make you call bullshit."

Wren had to know. "Try me."

"I think you're the closest thing to perfect that I've seen in a long time, and it has nothing to do with your looks." Even as Haven said one of the nicest things Wren had ever heard, his expression never changed. He didn't look like a man saying whatever it took to get a piece of ass. Haven looked like they talked about the weather and could keep up their chat all day.

Wren ran his hands up Haven's chest. He let his fingers enjoy some play time with Haven's chest hair, but his gaze never wavered from Haven's face. "Do you like to kiss?"

"I like everything the least bit carnal."

Wren's mouth lifted in one corner against his will. He hadn't been lying earlier. Wren liked Haven. "Is it okay if I kiss you?"

A smile exploded across Haven's face, stealing Wren's breath. "Are you waiting for me to beg?"

A wave of weariness washed over Wren. He shook his head. "I'm savoring a moment of absolute peace. It doesn't happen often that I get to stop being Sparrow and breathe." Wren couldn't believe he admitted that. It wouldn't happen again. He leaned forward and touched his lips to Haven's. Wren didn't try to deepen their kiss. For a moment, he simply lingered, taking his time. His lips parted. Wren sucked Haven's bottom lip, enjoying its plump texture. He nibbled, wanting a taste. Still, Haven stayed completely still with his hands resting on Wren's thighs. He teased Haven into kissing him back. Their tongues stroked, slow and perfect. It was sweet. Something shifted in Wren's chest. He pulled away and dropped his forehead to Haven's sternum. With his eyes closed, Wren shifted positions, until he was leading Haven's cock to his asshole. He rocked, taking Haven inside a little at a time. Wren no longer knew who he tortured—Haven or himself. All he knew was Haven let him be completely in charge, so he took advantage. He let Haven fill him while thrusting at the perfect angle. Wren didn't think about Haven's pleasure at all. He found the perfect rhythm, ensuring Haven's dick pounded right where Wren wanted. With his eyes closed and his mind firmly locked on finding release, Wren used Haven's body like an inanimate toy. Occasionally, Haven gasped or moaned, but he mostly let Wren enjoy him uninterrupted. It was freeing and empowering. Haven didn't weigh him down with expectation. He silently took what Wren gave. Nothing in his life had ever made him want to please someone else more. For every tiny sound he dragged from Haven, Wren fought to steal another. Pre-cum leaked from Wren, leaving a trail across Haven's stomach. As Wren's balls drew up tight, his pace quickened. Sounds of slapping skin filled the air, joining their struggles for breath. Haven still didn't give in to temptation. He remained completely still, letting Wren fuck himself on Haven's hard cock. Wren took complete advantage. He used the man's dick as rough as he wanted. Wren didn't hold back.

Pressure built. Wren bit and sucked at Haven's lips until the man gave up his tongue. Wren kissed Haven every bit as wildly as he fucked him. His muscles tightened in anticipation. Wren held his breath. The pressure on his crown grew until insanity scratched at Wren's brain. A cry tore from his lips and vibrated through their kiss as cum coated Haven's chest. Still, he didn't stop trying to take Haven's cock as deep as possible. He felt Haven's muscles spasm beneath him, but Haven didn't make a sound. Even as he joined Wren in oblivion, Haven didn't make the moment about him. Wren leaned away and stared down at Haven. He had to watch as Haven rode the height of orgasm. Haven was flushed and beautiful. He looked like Wren had taken him somewhere good. Someplace where life didn't hurt. Wren was moved by him. He hoped they crossed paths again, even if they never touched again. Sometimes, it was nice to dream that someone could love him.

WREN HAD FALLEN ASLEEP ON HIS CHEST AND Haven tried his ass off not to feel anything. He was probably the most intense, controlling, and possessive person on the planet. His heart made all sorts of noises with Wren curled against him, getting sleep that was obviously needed more than anyone realized. Haven squeezed his eyes shut and slipped from beneath Wren. He moved slow, determined not to disturb him. His entire soul screamed for him to stay. That was exactly why Haven needed to go. The only way he knew how to be a good person was to do the opposite of what he wanted. He wanted Wren. As he watched Wren sleep, Haven accepted that truth. What he had thought was sexual desire turned out to be more. Haven cared. No one deserved that.

After tearing his gaze away, Haven gathered his things and headed down the hall. This time, he focused on his surroundings. While Wren's house wasn't huge, it was gorgeous and screamed love. It was obvious Wren had done everything possible to make his home handicap accessible, even though Finch didn't live here. The expense he had gone to for Finch blew Haven away. The van alone had to have cost a fortune, considering how infrequently is was probably used. Wren did that out of love. This place, that van, and Finch's obviously expensive wheelchair were the real reason Wren worked like he did. Haven imagined, since Finch wasn't Wren's child, the state probably covered most of his actual care, but Wren made his life whole. Wren was the reason he had the best of everything. He humbled Haven. In all his life, Haven had never witnessed something so pure as Wren's love and sacrifice. He needed to get out of the way before he somehow destroyed all of this.

He dressed as quietly as possible while standing in the middle of Wren's kitchen. Everything was silent other than the slight hum of his refrigerator. The place was spotless—like Wren was never there.

The white cabinets didn't have a speck of dust or dirt. His black refrigerator and cooktop stove didn't have a smudge. Haven wondered what it must be like to have a life so completely opposite of his. He was always home. Alone.

Haven found his phone and pulled up Tucker's number. Not only was he the Kodiak brother Haven had known the longest, he was the only one who hadn't shown any hostility toward Haven after Haven's meltdown. Tucker was the only person Haven felt comfortable calling for help. He headed out as he put the phone to his ear. Haven didn't want to risk talking inside and waking Wren. His call was answered on the second ring.

"Hey, did you get lost on the trip to take Finch home?"

Haven sat on Wren's front steps. "No. Wren was really upset after dropping off Finch. He needed a minute and fell asleep. I don't want to wake him, but I'm stuck at his place now. Is there any way—"

"I'll come get you," Tucker said, cutting him off. "I've got Wren's address on file. Give me about ten minutes."

"Thank you." Tucker had no idea how much Haven appreciated the save.

"No problem. See you in a few."

"Yeah. See you." Haven disconnected the call and stared at nothing. All he saw was Wren's face. He wanted to feel something—some shattering remorse for moving on. Wren was the first person Haven slept with since losing Kevin. Haven had broken every silent vow he had made about staying alone forever, and he had done it for Wren. It seemed there should be some stabbing pains in his chest or something. Haven felt nothing. That wasn't entirely true. There was an overwhelming need sitting on his throat, choking him. His skin crawled with the desire to rush back inside, kiss Wren awake, and steal everything from him. But Haven stayed still and waited for Tucker, because that was the right thing to do.

By the time Tucker arrived, Haven forced himself to measure his every step. He wanted to run to the truck and jump in, speeding away in the opposite direction of temptation. Instead, he walked at a normal pace. Haven concentrated on smiling as he climbed into the passenger seat.

"Hey. Thanks again," he said, keeping his gaze locked on putting on his seatbelt.

Tucker pulled away from the curb. "It's no problem. I'm glad you called. Loyal was worried about Wren."

Haven snorted. "I'm not that bad of a person. Never mind. Yes, I am."

"It didn't have anything to do with you," Tucker said, sounding slightly annoyed. "He said Wren looked brittle by the end there, and he worried Wren might fall apart."

With his gaze locked on the road, Haven nodded. "That's why I took his keys. It was pretty heartbreaking."

"Damn, he's amazing, though, isn't he?" The awe in Tucker's words couldn't be missed.

Haven swallowed—hard. He fought the urge to tell Tucker to turn around. Take him back. "He definitely makes me wish I was a better human." Haven had no clue how he managed to sound so normal. Minutes passed in silence before Tucker snorted, bringing Haven's gaze his way. "What?"

Tucker shook his head a chuckled. "I was just thinking. Maybe we should change our company name to Cubs for Rent to Own." Tucker laughed harder.

Haven's eyebrows tried crawling up into his hairline. "Why?"

Laughing eyes flashed Haven's way before Tucker went back to watching the road. "Because everyone who signs up to work for us finds love.

We're more of a dating site than we ever intended to be."

Haven shrugged. "That's not entirely true. I'm still single."

Tucker snorted so hard, it sounded like it hurt. "Dude. I think you should drop that sun visor over there and take a look in the mirror. It couldn't be more obvious you got fucked today. Your hair is standing in every direction and your lips are swollen. Plus, there is a hickey on your neck that definitely wasn't there earlier. Not to mention, you spent the entire day staring a hole in the side of Wren's head. I'm surprised you managed to find your mouth when you ate. If you want to pretend you're not completely obsessed with the guy, you need to polish your acting skills."

Rather than calling Tucker a liar, Haven chose to focus on the dashboard. He turned inward. His lips did still tingle from Wren's biting kisses and Haven hadn't thought to check his hair. He had been so intent on getting the hell out of there, Haven hadn't been thinking at all. "I'm a bad person." Haven didn't mean to say the words aloud, but they were true nonetheless.

Tucker didn't laugh. Instead, when he spoke, he sounded like he took Haven seriously. "Wren doesn't strike me as someone who does anything on anyone else's terms. I think it's safe to say he wouldn't have touched you if he didn't want to."

Haven's gaze slid Tucker's way. "It doesn't have anything to do with Wren. I was a bad person long before I met him. Do you think people can change?"

Tucker didn't answer right away—like he gave Haven's question some real thought before responding. "I think people can and do change all the time. For the better and for the worse. Life is full of bullshit that makes and breaks people all day long. Sometimes, we change because we're determined to be better. Other times, life kicks your legs out from beneath you, leaving you no choice but to change course." Tucker flashed him an understanding smile. "The first step is self-discovery. It's obvious you care about Wren and you want to be better. The only advice I can give you is to treat him like a hat and never stop."

Haven blinked. Despite everything, a smile tugged at his lips. Sometimes, Tucker was ridiculous. "What the fuck does treat him like a hat mean?"

A dimple appeared in Tucker's cheek a half second before he flashed Haven a bright smile. "Chase after him if he gets carried away, pick him up if he falls, and give him lots of head."

A burst of laughter escaped Haven without warning. He thought there might be some decent advice somewhere in that completely ludicrous speech. If not, Haven still felt better. Tucker hadn't told him he was crazy for even considering living again. That was something. Now all Haven had to do was convince himself, and Wren, that he wasn't a complete waste of space. The odds were pretty slim on that one.

FOUR

"YOU'RE BEING VERY QUIET TONIGHT."

Wren forcibly pulled his thoughts away from Haven at Dex's claim. He knew it was true. "Sorry, gorgeous. I don't know where I went for a minute."

Dex wasn't one to care enough to look for a lie in Wren's words. "It's fine. I'm just not used to you being anything but the brightest star in the room."

That was uncharacteristically nice. Wren turned off his brain. "Are you feeling neglected, sexy? Let's see," Wren said, casting a look around the crowded set. "Which of these men do you have your cock set on winning? Don't answer yet. I want to guess." He leaned closer to Dex while scanning the room. "You prefer blonds, obviously. Hmm. It's slim pickings this season."

"Yeah. There's no one," Dex said, sounding bummed. "For a hot minute, we had a bitchy little makeup artist, but he didn't last."

At Dex's bored-sounding complaint, Wren's smile turned genuine. Dex was a terrible person. Selfish and vain. Still, Wren had a soft spot for him. They understood each other. "It's for the best, I would think. A bitchy makeup artist sounds like a harassment suit in the making."

Dex's cold and cutting gaze slid Wren's way. "I've never coerced a single soul. You know they all come to me first."

"Yeah, I know," Wren said, waving off Dex's open irritation. "They fall at your feet. You make them beg. How boring."

"It really is," Dex said absently as he went back to watching the organized mayhem happening around them.

It wasn't uncommon for Dex to hire him for the day just to hang out on set. He liked keeping a close watch on his latest creation. This time, it was twenty college kids, living together on a ranch. They had to survive farmhand life with very little help from actual ranch hands beyond chastising them for screwing up. On top of their daily chores, they were given crazy tasks to complete to keep from getting voted out. Dex loved watching people turn on each other, especially spoiled sexy people.

Wren squeezed Dex's knee. "Well, sweetie. I've got another job to get to, unfortunately. Be sure to torment all the rich kids on my behalf."

Before Wren could slip away, Dex grabbed his hand and stood. He headed toward his trailer without a backward glance and dragged Wren along in his wake. Wren was used to it. He had learned a long time ago to just go along for the ride with Dex. He opened his trailer door and waved Wren inside the forty-eight-foot-long trailer that cost over a million dollars and kept Dex in style while he relaxed during filming. Wren had been inside the luxurious space countless times. He no longer noticed the wastefulness of it all.

Dex closed them inside. "I have a present for you."

That wasn't new, but it was unexpected. Wren didn't think he had done anything special lately to deserve anything extra. "Really?" Even to Wren's ears, he sounded wicked. Playing the rich man's toy was second nature to Wren.

The billionaire known as Dex Wise had perfected the bored playboy persona. He didn't quite smile at Wren's reaction, but he was pleased. Wren could always tell. That was how he had managed to secure this spot as the man's favorite. Dex snagged a gold-wrapped box off the kitchen counter. "Nothing in life is free, of course."

Of course. Wren lowered his lashes and bit back a smirk. "Hmmm. I wonder what this gift will cost me."

"A kiss."

"A kiss?" Wren couldn't have been more surprised if Dex punched him. Dex did not kiss anyone. Ever. He didn't like to kiss. In fact, Wren had once misread the man's cues and kissed him. It had not ended well. Dex hadn't stopped punishing him with the silent treatment for six weeks. He had kept hiring Wren, though, at his lowest fee, just so Wren didn't miss a moment of his punishment. In the end, he had explained they would never be kissing again. Wren had taken that lesson to heart. Now Dex was demanding a kiss. Wren didn't know how to react.

Dex looked one hundred percent serious. He held the present out to Wren. "I'll let you open the box and decide if it's worth the cost."

Wren didn't take it. "I'm confused."

For the first time in the two years Dex had been hiring him, Dex smiled. It looked real too. Wren was frozen in place. "This is a new look for you, fire sprite. I've never seen you off kilter. This gift-giving thing is a lot of fun." Dex took Wren's hand and wrapped his fingers around the box. "Open the box."

In a show of Herculean strength, Wren tore his gaze away from Dex's laughing eyes. He focused on the gift. With his brain still glitching, Wren pulled the bow loose and tucked it in his back pocket before lifting the lid from the box. Inside there was a stack of paperwork. A bad feeling crawled up Wren's spine as he pulled the paperwork out and set aside the box. He flipped through each document, doing his best to hide his reaction. Wren wasn't that strong. His vision blurred. A lump filled his throat, threatening to cut off oxygen to his brain.

"How did you do this?" The question came out sounding as wrecked as Wren felt.

"Money, my wicked boy. That's the only game in town when it comes right down to it. Tell me you love me and give me my kiss."

The room darkened around the edges of Wren's vision as he lifted his gaze to focus on Dex. "Why would you do this for me?"

Dex pulled a face. "Don't turn into *that* guy. You're a wild, exotic creature with the perfect amount of low morals and beauty to complement me

59

perfectly. We don't play games, fire sprite. In a perfect world, you wouldn't need someone with no scruples like me to ensure you got custody of Finch. If your father wasn't such a fucked-up prick, Finch would be getting the amazing care he deserves from the brother who loves him without me dropping half a mil on a judge I know, but this isn't that world." Dex invaded Wren's space. He looked intense and serious again—like the Dex that Wren knew. He stroked Wren's face. "You are my pet, and I take care of what's mine. Now tell me you love me and kiss me, so I know you like your gift."

The thing was, if Dex was any other man on the planet, Wren would be certain there were more strings than that. But it was Dex and he didn't care enough about anyone to bother with plucking strings. He had a wild hair and it just happened to benefit Wren. There was no way Dex fully comprehended the magnitude of the paperwork Wren held. He had never loved anyone. Dex wasn't capable of grasping how being given custody of Finch was the single most important thing on the planet to Wren. Wren set the paperwork aside by force of will alone. He wanted to hug those typed words to his chest for the rest of the night. Instead, he twisted his fingers around the tails of

Dex's expensive button-down shirt and lured him close. He held Dex's stare and paid the man's price.

"You are amazing, and I love you so much more than you could ever know." It was true. Wren did love Dex like a person loved their best friend, or—as Dex had described—like a pet loved its owner.

For a moment, Dex hesitated an inch from Wren's lips, making Wren wonder if he regretted his demands. Then Dex barely brushed his lips across Wren's in the lightest of chaste kisses before he leaned away. He looked calculating. "What if I asked you for something different instead?"

Fuck. It looked like Dex was in the mood for string plucking after all. "Like?" Wren kept his tone lighthearted. He could never forget his role.

"I'd like for you to quit The Woodshed. It's getting in the way of you spending your weekends with me. You know I'm greedy and that place is tiresome. I don't like tiresome things that cut into my fun." He brought Wren's hand to his chest. "You know I'm a very spoiled man. It's too late to go back now."

He wanted to say no, but those custody and promise of financial support papers were sitting there, taunting Wren. They weren't something Dex could take back. It was all legal now. Wren couldn't say no, and that was the most terrifying part.

Wren decided to push his luck a little. "I'll quit The Woodshed after tonight. I'm not the kind of person who doesn't show up when I'm scheduled. You know that's one of the reasons you adore me," Wren said, keeping his tone teasing.

Dex's chest expanded as if he took an irritated breath. "Okay. One more night." A mischievous glint entered his eyes. "Fuck it. I still want that kiss." That was all the warning he got before Dex's mouth covered his. There wasn't a single aspect of Dex that wasn't sexy and practiced. His kiss was no different. It was impressive, but something was missing. Wren had a bad feeling he knew exactly what it was—Dex wasn't Haven. That didn't stop Wren from pouring his heart into their kiss. Despite everything, Dex was the one person in his life who never abandoned him. That would change someday. One of these days, he would get bored and move along. For now, Wren was still the pet.

Dex pulled away and grabbed the paperwork Wren had set aside. He pressed into Wren's arms. "Get lost, fire sprite. I might change my mind about negotiating with you if you stick around."

Wren smirked and winked while trying to hide

how tightly he held the greatest gift he had ever received to his chest. "You know how to reach me." Wren let himself out without looking back. He didn't know how to show weakness, but he was barely holding his shit together. Wren wanted to sit in his car and read every word of what he held. He couldn't wait to tell Finch. Jesus. Wren never dreamed he would get custody of Finch. Not only was he young, his money was immorally earned. There was nothing about him that recommended him to the courts, except there was no one who loved Finch more. Wren barreled a path to his car, not bothering to look right or left.

"Excuse me. Hey. Hold up. God dang. For a little guy, you can move fast."

It took Wren a moment to realize he was the one being chased. A big cowboy in a black cowboy hat and boots was hot on his heels. Wren slowed. The guy was all smiles, dimples, and flashing blue eyes. Wren blinked at the sight of him. "Are you yelling for me?"

The guy slowed, holding something red in his hand. "You dropped this back there. I'm not sure if it's anything you care about, but still." He held the piece of material out to Wren.

Wren realized it was the ribbon he had shoved in

his back pocket. "Oh. Damn. Thank you." He relieved the guy of the scrap of material. Even though he didn't really care about the ribbon, the guy had chased him all the way outside.

The guy tipped his hat. "You're very welcome." He didn't go away.

Wren eased a step closer to his car. "So." He eyed the guy's outfit. Wranglers, boots, and button-down denim shirt. "Are you part of the show?"

"Unfortunately."

His answer surprised a laugh from Wren. He was damnably positive by nature. Wren couldn't help it. He had built his life on being sparkly. "Now I have to know. Why do you say it like that? You don't look like you're one of the contestants."

"No. Definitely not. I work here on the ranch, which I never thought would mean babysitting a horde of college-aged alcoholics." He immediately looked horrified. "You're not one of them, are you?"

Another bubble of laughter spilled out. He was making this guy so uncomfortable; it was adorable. "No. Definitely not." He shifted his things to one arm and held his hand out. "I'm Wren. No affiliation with the show whatsoever." He scrambled for a way to explain his presence. "I'm..."

"Here with Dex," the guy supplied. "I saw y'all together earlier. I'm Colt."

"Nice to meet you, Colt. Good luck with the babysitting. You never know, there might be some side benefits of working with a bunch of drunk college students."

Colt swept a subtle glance down Wren's body. Anyone else might have missed it, but drawing men's interest was literally his profession. "Nah. People like that don't tempt me in the least. What did you say you do?"

Wren fought a smile. "I didn't."

"How did you say I could reach you for dinner?"

Another laugh burst from Wren. He had to give Colt credit. The guy was funny and unpredictable.

"Wow. No one can say you don't know how to shoot your shot."

"Colt."

They both turned at the yell.

Dex stood, hands in pockets and glaring. "Wren is already late to work," Dex said the moment he had their attention.

Colt didn't rush away. In fact, he looked as if Dex's open hostility didn't mean shit to him as he focused on Wren once more. "I'm sorry. I didn't realize I was holding you up."

Wren flashed him a sweet smile. Colt seemed nice. "It's okay. This is my last night anyhow, but I had better head out before I land you on Dex's shit list."

Colt's huge shoulders lifted in a careless shrug. "Fuck that guy. I don't work for him. How about that dinner?"

Wren opened his car door. "It was really nice meeting you, Colt." The guy was a sexy bear, but Wren only touched one man for free. And that one had disappeared the moment he had gotten what he wanted, as he should have done.

"Wren."

Oops. Now Dex was yelling at him. Wren felt his smile hitch up a notch. This was a conundrum. Dex would eat Colt for breakfast, but Colt didn't look the least bit concerned. Wren's gaze moved Dex's way. "I'm going."

Dex nodded, sure in the knowledge Wren would obey. "Get in the car, pet."

"I do work for him," Wren said with an apologetic shrug. "And I'm a very obedient boy."

Colt still jumped to stop him from closing the door. "Then tell me one way I can find you without this guy interfering."

"I work for Cubs for Rent," Wren said last

minute before closing the door. He wouldn't risk angering Dex, and once Colt realized what Cubs for Rent was, he wouldn't want anything else to do with him. That was the way the world worked. It was best he enjoyed his quick flirt and moved along. Dex wasn't likely to forgive Colt this one, and Wren very much doubted Colt had ever had an enemy like Dex.

Haven waited until the exact time he had arrived last time to show up at The Woodshed. The place wasn't as bad as it sounded. While it was low lit and filled with exactly the type of people he expected to find, they also had a lot of ways to keep the dancers safe. Men danced in cages and on poles. Other men in even less clothing gave lap dances and god knew what else in dark corners. Haven wasn't here for any of that. He spotted Wren the moment he stepped inside, dancing in the same cage. This time, he wore a black leather thong, combat boots, and a black leather hat with silver studs. Just as last time, his body moved in perfect time with the music, flexing muscles in a show of strength that would make anyone jealous... or hot. Haven knew the exact moment he was spotted. A wicked smile stretched

Wren's lips, and Haven swore every move Wren made became all about him. When Haven made his way to the bottom edge of the cage, Wren went down on his knees, and continued his seductive dance.

"Are you getting attached, sexy?"

If Haven knew one thing, he knew Wren would not want that. "Maybe I'm not here for you. I think I might check out the rest of the guys."

Humor flashed in Wren's eyes. "Have fun then, gorgeous. I get off in ten."

Wren somehow managed to shift back to his feet and make it look like part of his routine. Men clamored to shove handfuls of bills between the bars, begging Wren to show them more skin. He teased them by two-handing his thong and flirting with the possibility of showing the whole package. Haven couldn't look away. He had seen the whole package and it was amazing. There wasn't much he wouldn't give to see it again.

Wren's gaze met his. His eyebrows rose—like asking if he wanted to see. Haven tapped his watch. The laughter written on Wren's face made Haven feel ten years younger. His cheeks ached, making him realize how big his smile had become. Just being in Wren's presence was enough for him. Haven motioned toward the back and Wren gave him a subtle nod. Since he felt sure Wren understood he would meet him outside like last time, he headed out. There was no one else there he cared to see.

Outside, Haven leaned against Wren's car and stared at the night sky. He wouldn't lie to himself. Haven couldn't claim he didn't know why he couldn't stay away. He hadn't realized how much he missed happiness until Wren brought it back into his life. For a moment, Haven fought the urge to text Kevin and apologize for the millionth time. This level of joy was what he had stolen from them. If Kevin felt this again with Jericho, Haven couldn't blame him for marrying Jericho as quick as he possibly could. That wasn't an option for Haven. He knew these stolen moments with Wren were just that. They wouldn't be some grand love story and that was okay. Haven just wanted some little piece of Wren's life, because he was so damn bright with inner light that even the tiniest bit of him was like an inferno. Haven was a moth. He couldn't resist the light.

The back door opened, and Wren stepped out. Haven was drawn toward him. His feet moved in Wren's direction like they had no other choice. The smile Wren wore was too hard to resist. "I wanted to explain about leaving while you were asleep the other day."

A line appeared between Wren's brows. "I don't give a fuck about that, but guess what?"

He was amazing. "What?"

Wren hurriedly pulled his keys from his pocket and unlocked his car door. Haven watched his sexy ass while he rummaged around inside before coming out with a huge stack of papers. He held the up proudly—like showing off a prized possession. "Look. I got custody of Finch." His huge grin said all Haven needed to know about how much that meant.

He did his best to match Wren's happiness level and show his support. "That's the best news I've heard in ages. Wow. What does that mean for y'all now?"

Wren twisted the pages and eyed them before shrugging. "Not much right away, except I can keep him overnight now, and once we've gone through some classes and he's better adjusted, maybe he can come live with me."

"Oh my god," Haven said, realizing how much this meant to Wren. "That's fantastic. Is Finch excited?"

Wren set the papers back inside his car. "I don't know. I just found out tonight, so I haven't had time to tell him yet. Would you like to go with me tomorrow to tell him?"

"Sure. That sounds great." Actually, it sounded like Wren might need him if things didn't go well, but whatever.

"I want to celebrate. Let's go do something."

Haven shrugged. "Sure. What would you like to do?"

"Let's go dancing. I know I dance all night, but I'm so excited. My heart is racing, and I need to work off the extra energy. Do you like to dance?"

Not really. "I haven't done it in a long time, but this is your night. Do I need to follow you somewhere?"

Wren nodded. "Let's go to my place first, so I can shower and change."

"Sounds good. I'll see you there."

Wren snagged the front of Haven's t-shirt before he could get away. "One thing before you go." He hauled Haven close and went up on his toes before pressing his lips to Haven's. Haven's hands automatically reached for Wren's ass, pulling him closer. He deepened their kiss. Passion exploded as he fought to taste every part of Wren's mouth. Last time, Wren had been in control. While things needed to stay that way, Haven wanted this kiss badly. Still, he forced himself to take a step back. Wren's bottom lip called to him. Haven swiped his thumb across it, enjoying the way his soft flesh felt.

"Drive safe. I'll be right behind you."

The way Wren nodded, looking dazed, made Haven fight an evil grin. Maybe Haven was a terrible mess, but he knew how to please. "See you soon."

Haven waited until Wren was safely locked inside his car before sliding behind the wheel of his BMW X6. He followed Wren from the lot, doing his best not to think. Haven refused to believe he was falling under Wren's spell. They were only friends. That was all they could be. By the time he sat parked in Wren's driveway, he had almost convinced himself that was true. Then he followed Wren inside, and the truth grew larger alongside his hunger.

Wren glanced over his shoulder as they moved through the kitchen. "I'll just jump in the shower." He peeled his dark t-shirt over his head and set it on the counter. Haven barely spared the clothing a glance. His gaze ate up Wren's body, sliding down his perfect spine and watching as his jeans loosened at the waist. "You can join me if you're interested." His jeans slipped lower, teasing Haven with a hint of crack and cheek. Haven didn't agree but neither did he stop moving. His dick was already hard, and his palms itched to touch Wren again.

Wren headed inside the bathroom in his bedroom. Haven stopped short of crossing that threshold. Instead, he veered left to the bedside table. While listening to the shower fire to life, Haven stripped before digging a condom from the drawer. He rolled the sheath down his length. His hunger grew by the second as his feet carried him inside the bathroom.

He could see Wren's beautiful nude body through the clear shower door. With his head down, Wren let the water cascade down his body. Many times in his life, Haven had been scared of his desires. He knew he felt things deeper and stronger than most and his feelings poured out in the unhealthiest ways. Wren was so independent. He didn't need anyone, and that knowledge changed something in Haven. Haven still felt the need to overwhelm Wren's life until he couldn't see anyone else, but the desire to bend Wren to his will wasn't there. It was like he had accepted that an impossible task, or Wren's independence was so damn beautiful, Haven didn't want to break it. No matter the reasons, Haven wanted Wren exactly as he was.

Wren didn't look his way as Haven joined him. Instead, he took a step back, moving into Haven's hold like the move had been choreographed. Haven's teeth found Wren's shoulder. He nipped as his hand slid down the front of Wren's body. His fingers curled around Wren's erection and tugged.

A soft moan bounced from the walls of the shower, caressing Haven's ears. His entire body ached with need. Haven's hips rolled like they had a mind of their own, thrusting against Wren's tight round ass. Wren's spine arched. A pant escaped Haven. Haven stroked Wren's cock like he pleasured himself. Wren moved against him, as if incapable of being still. Haven found himself fucking Wren's crack. It felt ridiculously good to have his erection trapped between their bodies.

He lightly held Wren's throat with one hand while he jacked him off with the other, keeping Wren exactly where he wanted him. "You asked me last time if I thought you would be exciting." Haven bit Wren's neck, savoring the man with every sense—Wren's touch, his taste, his smell, the way his moans sounded in the tiny shower, and the sight of his sexy body. "I thought you would be just like this—perfect in my arms. When you come and you're shaking with aftershocks, I'm going to fuck you. I don't plan to be gentle, so back down now if you can't handle that."

A loud gasp escaped Wren, and his cock jerked in Haven's hand, bringing an evil smile to Haven's face as he realized Wren had orgasmed at his words. He had known Wren liked it rough. Haven could give him what he needed. With the slightest urging, Haven had Wren bent over and was shoving his way inside. The lubricated condom was all he had to ease the way. Wren's tight ass tried sucking him deeper. Moans echoed around them, mixing with the sound of Haven's hips slapping against Wren's wet ass. Water poured down their bodies as Haven held Wren's hips and thrust hard enough to lift Wren's feet from the floor. Nothing existed but them. Haven had one goal—orgasm. Wren felt amazing on his dick and Haven needed oblivion. He already knew once wouldn't be enough. Haven just needed to take the edge off before he spent the rest of the night playing with Wren's body. His brain itched. He needed to come. Pressure was climbing up his erection while madness clawed at his insides. Wren was sexy and responsive. He made Haven want to live inside him. Without warning, pleasure sucker-punched him in the gut. A cry tore from his lips as his body shook. Wave after wave of ecstasy had him pumping deep, trying to savor every sensation to the very end. Haven didn't want to stop. He wanted to feel like this forever with Wren. When his dick slipped from Wren's ass, he gasped at how sensitive everything felt. He needed Wren's dick in his mouth. Haven wanted cum on his tongue.

He swept Wren off his feet and into his arms. "I'm sorry. You can finish your shower later. Right now, I need to suck you off like I need my next breath." That was all the explanation he offered before carrying a wet and willing Wren to bed.

WREN'S ENTIRE BODY HUMMED WITH PLEASURE. He could still feel every place Haven had been. Even though the storm had passed, there was still a tugging in his chest, saying they weren't done for the night. Wren stared at their linked fingers as he did his best to get his palm as flat as possible against Haven's. "Before I forget to tell you, tonight was my last night at The Woodshed."

Haven cocked his head to one side, as if trying to get a better look at Wren's face. "What made you decide that?"

Wren shrugged. "I'll probably regret it, but I

need to be free. You know, in case a higher bidder wants to hire me or whatever. I make more money with Cubs for Rent. Plus, I don't want to tell Finch no if he asks to stay the night. Can I ask you a question?" Wren asked before Haven could dig deeper.

"Of course."

"What made you decide to do demos for something you no longer practice?"

Haven didn't answer right away, making Wren wonder if he was trying to think of a lie. "When Orion first suggested it, I was ready to hard pass. It's all parlor tricks, you know. I only demo the light, fluffy stuff, which I didn't figure anyone would really pay to see. Originally, I put together a fun little show for book conventions to make sure readers enjoyed themselves and to sell books. I honestly thought doing big parties for the rich would be a disaster. But..." Haven hesitated to the point Wren almost pinched him. He took a deep breath. It sounded almost painful. "But then, I found out my ex-husband was hiring guys from the same company to go on dates with him. So, for lack of any way to make myself look better in this story, I decided to accept because I knew he would be tripping over me everywhere he went."

"Ex-husband." Wren didn't know why he dragged the words out. "Wow." Wren cleared his throat. He had no room to be upset. "Were you hoping to hurt him or tempt him with what he was missing?"

He felt Haven shrug. Haven brought their joined hands to his lips and kissed Wren's knuckles. "Neither, really. I guess I hoped if he kept seeing my face, then he would come back."

That was something Wren could see himself doing. If he wanted someone, he would make damn sure they saw his face everywhere they went. "Since you're here, I'm guessing it hasn't worked so far."

"I'm here because I don't want to be anywhere else," Haven said, licking Wren's wrist. "But, no. It didn't work. He got remarried a few weeks ago." Before Wren could comment, Haven nearly shocked him speechless. "To Loyal's dad."

"Whoa. Your ex married Jericho?" Damn. That dude was hot. They had met when Dex had hired Jericho for the night. It hadn't gone well from what Wren had heard from Dex. Of course, Wren thought that was probably bullshit. Dex had been punishing Wren for being late for their last date. So he had hired someone else. Of course, afterward, Dex had called Wren and made things right... the way he always did. Still, Jericho was hot. Wren liked Haven better, though. "That still doesn't explain why you don't practice what you teach."

Haven made a humming noise that had Wren pressing his ear harder against Haven's chest trying to feel the sound. His fingers trailed down Wren's spine. "I'm cutting a cancer from myself and maybe some good things are going with the mass, but this is the only chance I have of getting well."

Wren understood that more than Haven knew. Maybe Haven needed to know he wasn't alone. "Before my dad died, Finch was little, and it was just the two of us all the time. I didn't realize how bad things were financially or how far gone my dad was because we never saw him. The house slowly got emptier, but I had never had to pay for anything in my life, so I was blind to it all. I didn't realize things were getting sold off to pay for our care while Dad drained the accounts. Then he was gone." Wren swallowed hard at the memory. "Losing him meant nothing really, since he was never around. It wasn't like when Mom died. Losing her was ugly, but I got Finch in the deal and it was like he was my baby." A smile pulled at the corners of his mouth. "I was only eight, but he was so tiny, and Dad didn't want much to do with him. Looking back, I think Dad blamed

Finch for her death. He saved me, though. Finch loved me when I needed it most. Maybe he didn't know any better, since I was the only person taking care of him, but still—to me—he was mine. Next thing I knew, I was sixteen, Dad was dead, and they were taking Finch away. No one wanted him but me, but I wasn't old enough to keep him, nor did I have the funds to care for him. They auctioned Dad's house and every penny went to the home for Finch's care. There was nothing I could do but lose him." Damn, the memory hurt every bit as much as if it happened yesterday. "There was nothing I wouldn't have done to make sure he had every comfort in a place where he didn't have me. He was scared and didn't understand why I wouldn't take him home. I just felt sick and helpless all the time. There was one thing I had, though, and I found out real fast what men would do to have it." Wren motioned absently down his body. "Unfortunately, I had been every bit as sheltered as I kept Finch. But like you said, I had a cancer inside me—innocence and shame. I had to carve it from my heart and harden myself so I could survive. Some good things got lost in the mix, though," Wren added, sounding absent even to his ears. Wren stared at nothing, trying to feel nothing. Some days, it was harder than others.

Haven rolled, pinning Wren beneath him. As Haven's tongue brushed his, Wren's fingers found Haven's hair. Everything else disappeared. It didn't matter how they had ended up here or why they entertained each other. Wren didn't feel so inhuman when they were together. He couldn't afford to entertain this weakness forever, but surely one more night would be fine.

FIVE

AFTER THE FIFTH time of nervously cracking his fingers, Haven reached over and took Wren's hand. He brought it to his lips and placed tiny kisses across the back as he turned into the parking lot of Finch's home.

"It's fine, angel. You don't have any reason so be so nervous."

Wren flashed him a pained smile but didn't respond. In truth, Haven's nerves were completely frayed because Wren's were. He got it. Wren had spent the last two years trying to get custody of Finch and now the time was here. Haven couldn't imagine what they had been through.

With a final deep breath, Wren hugged the bear he had bought for Finch to his chest and stepped from the car. He walked to the front door, looking like a man walking to his death. Haven rushed ahead of him and opened the door. Before they made it ten steps inside, a middle-aged woman rushed into the hall. "Wren. Hey." She was all smiles. "The girls and I were hoping we could come with you if that's okay? Everyone has been dying to see Finch's reaction when he gets the news."

Wren looked like he would puke. Still, he smiled. "Of course, Mandy. All of you fought as hard for this as I did." Wren waited patiently as the women from the office rushed into the hall to join them. They moved as a group and Haven brought up the rear. He had no reason to be here other than Wren asking him to come. At the door that obviously led to Finch's room, Haven watched Wren take a breath and become someone else. It was like he flipped a switch and the fear was gone. He knocked lightly and then opened the door a few inches to peek in.

"It's the best big brother," Finch said so loudly, the words floated into the hall.

One of the women from the office covered her mouth and they all exchanged smiling glances. They all squeezed in around the door to watch without intruding. By the time Haven got close enough to see, Finch was already hugging his bear.

Wren held up the paperwork in Finch's direction. "Do you know what this is?"

"No." Finch had a breathy voice that made him sound excited, or maybe he really was excited. Haven couldn't tell.

"It's a whole bunch of words together, but they all add up to one thing. A judge has finally agreed that you're mine."

"No way."

Haven bit his bottom lip. His cheeks ached.

"Yes way," Wren said cheerfully. "Do you know what this means? It means, for now, you can come stay the night with me occasionally, and eventually—when you're ready—you can come live with me, if you want."

"No way." Finch released a loud squeal that bordered on ear piercing. Wren didn't even flinch then hugged him. Haven had to look away. He realized everyone else felt the same. All the women were wiping their eyes and fanning their faces. Haven swallowed-hard. He hadn't expected to be so moved, but he cared. Haven hadn't realized how small and self-centered life had been before meeting Wren. He hadn't known what it was like to sacrifice everything—to love someone more than he loved himself. Wren lived that reality every day. He deserved to have this one good thing. Haven blinked, coming back to himself as Wren stepped out in the hall. He focused on Mandy. "Did you already get a copy of all this paperwork?"

Mandy nodded. "Everything came yesterday along with a check from Mr. Wise for Finch's care. Everything is all good on our end. I can't tell you how happy we are for you two." Mandy fanned her face. "It still feels like yesterday... well, you know. I swear I can still hear his screams each time you left. This could not have happened soon enough for everyone involved."

Haven couldn't even blink as he watched the exchange. Apparently, this miracle was thanks to Dex Wise, and the man was also paying for Finch's care now. Fuck. A ton of reality slammed down on Haven. He cared about this guy. Haven cared about Wren and Wren would never be free to feel the same. If this was life testing him, it had picked one hell of a challenge. Haven was trying to be different, but maybe he didn't have this much change in him. He would keep his heart out of it and walk away when Wren told him to go. Wren belonged to Finch and Dex. Haven was just someone who felt more than he had been invited to feel. He had caught an unintentional glimpse beneath Wren's mask and wanted what he saw. None of that mattered. Wren's life had been hard before Haven had stormed in. If Haven saw he made it harder, he would stop.

Wren's gaze moved his way. A sweet smile touched his lips and he took Haven's hand, leading him inside the room. Haven followed, stepping even farther into Wren's world. He prayed he didn't fuck things up.

WHILE WATCHING FINCH KICK HAVEN'S ASS IN video games, Wren rode the high of things going so well. He knew they still had mountains. Finch wouldn't be coming home with him tomorrow, and—when he did—it might be much harder than Wren remembered. Still, for the first time in a long time, Wren thought things might work out for them.

Damn, Haven looked sexy laughing with Wren's brother. It was nice having Haven around. He had never really had any friends. Wren had gone to school online so he could take care of Finch and hadn't bothered finishing after his dad died. He had kind of disappeared between the cracks of the system and slid into the role of being for sale. Until Mister Haven had appeared in his life, Wren hadn't realized

anything was missing. Not really. Now he just felt...
something.

Wren glanced at the clock. It was getting late.
They had ordered dinner from a delivery app and
Haven had been playing every game Finch wanted
for hours. Really, it was just a bunch of button
mashing, but it made Finch happy and the nurses
swore it helped him with his fine motor skills. Still,
Wren needed to let Finch and Haven rest.

"Last round, guys. Haven's thumbs are probably
ready to fall off by now."

Haven chuckled but didn't confirm or deny
Wren's statement.

Finch gave a head bob that was his version of a
nod. "Yeah. He needs practice. I beat him every
time."

Wren snorted and crossed the room. He set
Finch's controllers aside and stole a hug. "Ugh, I hate
leaving you."

"I know. You always come back, though."

"That's right," Wren said fiercely. "Nothing
could keep me away. I love you, sweetie." He kissed
Finch's cheek while Finch tried kissing him back.
"Do you want anything else before I go? Do you
want me to help you change or anything?"

"No. I'm not tired." He hugged his new bear and

rubbed it against his cheek. "Ms. Suzie works tonight. She's teaching me to paint on a computer. I'm making something for you."

Wren's chest swelled with love. "I can't wait to see it. I'll be back tomorrow, and we'll go to the park. Okay?"

Finch tried to nod again. "Okay. I love you, best brother."

Wren smiled and kissed him again. "I love you too, sweet angel." Wren straightened to find Haven waiting patiently with his hands shoved in his pockets.

He smiled and nodded at Finch. "I had a great time, buddy. Let me get some practice in and I'll be ready for you next time."

"You need more practice than that," Finch said with a loud laugh. "Hugs before you go."

Haven looked surprised, but he changed places with Wren and hugged Finch.

"Love you, buddy," Finch said, shocking the hell out of Wren.

Wren covered his mouth.

Haven didn't bat an eye. "Love you too. See you soon."

Wren moved Finch's cellphone from the bedside table to the tray on his wheelchair to give himself something to do other than flip the fuck out. "Here you go. You text me if you need anything at all. You know I'm always only a call away."

Finch patted his hand, and Wren knew he was struggling to keep talking. Sometimes muscles just didn't cooperate when Finch needed them. He stole one more kiss and whispered his love before taking Haven's hand and leading him to the door. Wren held his silence until they were back inside Haven's car. That was when his feelings burst out. Before Haven could start the car, Wren snagged his collar and crawled across the center console. He captured Haven's mouth with all the intensity of everything he felt but couldn't explain. Haven didn't know. Wren had always been alone. He didn't feel alone anymore.

"Thank you," Wren whispered between kisses while doing his damnedest to squeeze into Haven's lap. "You're amazing." He kissed Haven deep, pouring his soul into it. "Thank you for being so amazing. Let me do something for you in return."

Haven cupped his face and held Wren away. His stare looked intense, more like the Dom and less like Haven than Wren had ever seen. "You are doing something for me in return. You're giving me your friendship and sharing your family with me. I don't have either of those things without you."

Haven's words squeezed Wren's heart. "You have friends. The Kodiak boys seem to love you."

There was a deep sadness in Haven's eyes as he shook his head. "I fucked that up months ago—like I do everything. Now, they tolerate me and that's about it. You're the only one who's ever happy to see me."

"Why don't you have a family?"

Haven's thumbs stroked Wren's cheeks. A sad smile touched his lips. "That's a much longer story. If you buckle up, I'll tell you about it on the way home."

Since Wren really wanted to know, he moved back to his seat and snapped his seatbelt in place.

Haven started the car and put it in reverse. He didn't speak again until they were on the road. "I ran away when I was fifteen."

Wren waited for more, but Haven didn't say anything else. A chuckle burst from Wren when he realized Haven didn't intend to say more. "Is that it?"

Haven smiled. A dimple appeared in his cheek. "No. I just kind of spaced as I realized I don't know where to start. There were so many things that I hated about my parents and about being a kid.

Honestly, I'm not sure how to vocalize it all. We fought always. About everything. There was always anger and slamming doors. I just wanted it to be quiet. It was exhausting. Half of the time, I didn't even understand why we were yelling at each other. It was like our personalities just clashed in every way. So, one day, I took all my books out of my backpack and hid them under some clothes in my closet. I stuffed the bag full of money, food, and a couple changes of clothes, and then I headed out for the bus stop like I did every morning. Except I kept going instead. I bought a bus ticket to San Antonio."

"Bought a bus ticket from where?" Wren wanted every detail.

"Comfort, Texas," Haven answered before moving on. "My history class had taken a field trip to The Alamo a month earlier and we were allowed to walk to the mall food court for lunch before returning to school. I was a loner, so I made my way over there by myself. On the way, this boy about my age stopped me. Honestly, I think he planned to rob me, but instead, we talked. He was homeless and lived with a huge group of teenagers in some old abandoned warehouse. They ran scams and picked pockets. None of them looked worse for the wear. I gave him my cellphone number, since he said he sometimes had access to cheap pay as you go phones." Haven shrugged. "I didn't really think I would hear from him again."

"But you did," Wren guessed. "And he sold you on the freedom of his life."

Haven flashed him a quick smile before going back to watching the road. "Pretty much."

"And you never saw your parents again?" Even Wren heard the disbelief in his voice. He knew how easy it was to fall through the cracks when a teen didn't have parents, but Haven had people. Most likely, he had people who had never stopped looking for him.

"Nope. I never saw them again." Haven said the words absently—like he thought about that a lot. "I met my ex-husband right after I turned eighteen and he became my family. I never looked back." Haven leaned his way and linked fingers with Wren.

Wren's curiosity was not assuaged. "Have you ever considered calling them or anything?"

Haven brought Wren's hand to his mouth and kissed it before holding it to his chest. He was slow to answer, but he sounded unmoving when he did. "No. When I married Kevin at twenty, applying for a marriage license triggered my social security number in the system and the police showed up at our house a few weeks after our wedding. They questioned me about my whereabouts for the previous five years and then warned me they would have to inform my parents I'd been found, and that my case had been closed. For weeks afterward, I expected them to show up at our door any minute. They never did." Wren couldn't tear his gaze away from Haven's face. His heart hurt as he watched a sardonic smile touch Haven's lips. "I'd always believed in my heart they'd been relieved once I was gone. That hadn't really hurt, though, until they didn't show, and I realized I was right. I make people tired, angel."

A swell of anger and possessiveness grew inside Wren until it filled him with some unnamed emotion. "No." The denial burst from Wren with all the fury he felt on Haven's behalf. "Those are your parents. If they didn't come for you, then they're bad people. Nothing could keep me from Finch. There is nothing he could ever do that would make me never see him again. If he went missing, I would scour the streets. I would never give up. If they don't want you, then they never deserved to have you." Even Wren heard the over-the-top conviction in his voice. He couldn't help it. He was outraged. Wren kind of wanted to track down Haven's parents and kick their asses.

"Your anger is adorable."

Haven's quietly spoken words had Wren deflating. Heat filled his cheeks. "Sorry. I guess I'm passionate about... things."

Haven put the car in park outside Wren's garage. He met Wren's gaze. "I get it, baby. You think everyone should love their children the way you love Finch. The thing is, not everyone is good like you."

He wasn't good. Not in the least. But it was nice having someone feel that way about him, and Wren didn't want to disabuse him of the notion. Wren wasn't sure what he wanted exactly. He just didn't want Haven to go away. "Would you like to stay the night?"

"There's nothing I'd rather do."

There should have been warning bells or something when Wren met Haven. It seemed crazy for such an innocuous moment out of time to have made such an impact on his life. Hell, after their first dinner, Haven had insulted him. There were so many reasons why he shouldn't have ended up here, but Wren wanted Haven in his life. If there was any mercy in the world, this wouldn't blow up in his face. He needed Haven to be something good.

SIX

WREN: *I'm nervous. One of my conditions for moving Finch in with me is taking this class. We have to go together so they can teach me to do some of the things his nurses do.*

Haven: *Why are you nervous about it? You're great with him.*

Wren: *What if they see how incompetent I am and decide I can't keep him after all?*

Haven: *Not possible. Finch couldn't be in better hands than yours.*

———

HAVEN: *I HAVE FOUR DEMOS TONIGHT. WHAT about you?*

Wren: *Date with Dex.*

Haven: *Naturally. Have fun... just maybe not too much fun.*

Haven: *Forget I said that. I had no right.*

Wren: *Hush. You have nothing to worry about. Come over after?*

Haven: *Definitely.*

Wren: *Would you like to stay the weekend with me?*

Haven: *I can't this weekend. I have a book conference. Would you like to go? It's in New Mexico.*

Wren: *I can't go out of town right now. I can't miss any of my visitation with Finch.*

Haven: *Sorry. I didn't think of that. I'll miss you.*

Wren: *Don't apologize. It's not your job to think of everything when it comes to me. I'll miss you too. Have fun... just maybe not too much fun.*

Haven: *You definitely have nothing to worry about. I'll see you when I get back.*

WREN: *FINCH IS SPENDING THE NIGHT FOR THE first time tonight. Yay! I'm scared as hell. What if something goes wrong and I panic? What if he doesn't feel safe and never wants to stay with me again?*

Haven: *None of that will happen, but I get it. This is important. Would you like me to stay with you, in case you need help?*

Wren: *Do you mind doing that? I would love you forever for the help.*

Haven: *Of course. I don't mind. Question, though. Did Finch bring his gaming system?*

Wren: *Yeah. I didn't want him to get bored.*

Haven: *Cool. I have an idea. I'll be there in thirty. Unless you want me to grab some pizza?*

Wren: *Finch is cheering about pizza. Extra cheese is his favorite.*

Haven: *I'm on it.*

Wren: *My hero.*

IT WASN'T THAT WREN THOUGHT HE COULDN'T handle Finch alone; he was just scared shitless something would go wrong. He needed this first night to be perfect. Haven came through the door, carrying pizza boxes and a plastic bag. Finch was practically dancing in his seat. His loud squeal rent the air, making Wren smile so hard, his face hurt. Finch adored Haven. It was heartwarming to have someone else in their lives.

Haven gave Wren a quick kiss as he set the pizza aside. As he kissed Finch's cheek, making sure he was included, something inside Wren shifted... melted.

Haven whipped a game from the bag with a flourish. "I stopped and got us this. It's a remastered game from my old gaming days. I thought, if you want, this might put us on a more level playing field."

"That sounds good because you need help."

Wren bit his bottom lip to keep from laughing. Finch had no filter. Wren snagged the pizza boxes. "I'll fix everyone a plate. The faster we eat, the faster you two can get your tournament started." Wren went to work getting his boys settled. His shoulders didn't completely relax until long after everyone had eaten, and he was kicked back in his leather recliner in danger of dozing.

Haven stood, making Wren jump and realize he had fallen asleep. "Okay, buddy. I think we better get ready for bed. Wren is snoring."

"I don't snore."

"Oh yes you do," Finch said, laughing.

"It's an adorable snore." The laughter in Haven's eyes didn't reassure Wren as much as it should.

Wren pushed to his feet. "All right. I'll quit assaulting everyone's ears. Come on, Finch. Let's get you ready for bed." He followed Finch down the hall and into his new bedroom. Finch had been overjoyed to see it when they had first gotten home. He had gone from one thing to another as fast as possible, checking out all his new stuff. Wren had been worried they would have a hard time at bedtime. It had been a long time since he had gone through the routine of getting Finch cleaned up and Finch was older now. Thankfully, being older meant a little more independent and things went much smoother than he imagined.

Wren tucked him into bed. "Take this," he said, handing Finch a remote that controlled the intercom system. "If you need anything, push the red button. Haven and I will be here at all times and one of us will be in here right away. Okay?"

Finch smiled. "I'll be okay. Love you both so much."

Until Finch included Haven in his claim, Wren didn't notice Haven hanging out in the doorway— like he was scared to come in without an invitation.

Wren waved him inside. "Come give goodnight hugs."

With a huge smile, Haven moved deeper into the room and gave Finch a hug. They exchanged kisses on the cheek while Wren stood with his heart in his throat. They were both so adorable. It was like they were a little family. Wren had to force himself to turn off the light and head to his room. Haven held his hand until the last second before Wren disappeared inside the bathroom to run through his nightly routine. Exhaustion weighed heavily on his shoulders by the time he moved back to the bed. A grateful smile tugged at his lips as he noticed Haven had already turned down the covers for him.

After a quick kiss, Haven took his turn in the bathroom while Wren settled in. The bed shifted beside him, making Wren realize he had drifted off again. Haven tugged Wren into his arms. Wren went willingly, using Haven's chest as a pillow. The sound of Haven's heartbeat and the way he softly rubbed Wren's back had Wren out like a light in two seconds.

"Haven." The whispered word through the intercom had Haven and Wren shooting up into a sitting position.

Haven clicked the button on the intercom. "What's up, buddy?"

"I'm scared." The whispered confession had Wren's heart twisting in his chest.

"Do you want me to send your brother in there?"

Finch kept whispering. "No. I don't want him to not invite me again. Can you come?"

Wren covered his mouth. His eyes burned. He was so damn grateful Haven had stayed the night. Otherwise, Finch might have been scared all night and not said anything.

"I'm on my way," Haven said, tossing back the covers. He switched off the intercom so Finch couldn't hear him before swiping his lips across Wren's. "Don't worry. I've got this."

Wren didn't doubt him at all. Still, he waited until Haven disappeared before setting the intercom on mute where he could listen in, but they couldn't hear him.

Haven's voice came through the speaker. "Are you okay?"

Finch's voice sounded small when he responded. "Yeah. It's a lot darker here."

"Let's do this." Wren listened to Haven shuffling around. "Is that better?"

"Yeah."

Haven's voice moved closer to the intercom, as if he had moved to stand over the bed. "Tell me what else I can do to make you feel secure. Is anything else out of place?"

"I don't like the closet."

"I'll block it closed with a chair for tonight, and then I'll put a sliding lock on it tomorrow so you can feel safe."

"Okay."

The legs of the chair scraped across the floor. Then Haven's voice was back. "Would you like for me to sit here with you until you fall asleep?"

"Yeah."

Wren blinked back tears at Finch's tiny voice and Haven's amazingness. He didn't know how to feel. More shuffling came through the intercom—like Haven settled in.

"Haven?"

"Yeah?"

"What if someone breaks in?"

"There's a really loud alarm that will sound and then I'll kick their ass." Wren bit back a chuckle at Haven's claim. "I won't let anyone hurt you." Wren's throat swelled. He was in love with Haven. There was no sense in lying to himself.

"Haven?"

"Yeah?"

"I love you."

"I love you too."

A tear slipped from the corner of Wren's eye and dropped onto the mattress. He swiped at his face. This was the life Wren wanted for Finch, and still it felt so out of permanent reach. He didn't know how to make anyone love him. Wren was a flirt and a tease. Those things he understood. This pressure on his chest, screaming he had to hang on to Haven, it was new and scary as hell. Haven wouldn't want Wren to keep dating for pay if they were a couple. Wren had no other choice. He didn't know if there was a middle ground. It was possible he would be alone again soon. Wren had to find a way to be okay with that.

WITH HIS FEET CROSSED AT THE ANKLES AND HIS arms crossed over his chest, Haven waited for Finch to fall asleep. The chair next to Finch's bed wasn't meant to be slept in and his neck screamed for a better position, but Haven wasn't moving until he knew Finch felt safe enough to sleep. A tiny snore came from the bed. A smile tugged at Haven's lips. It seemed Wren wasn't the only one with an adorable snore. He didn't move. Haven wanted Finch to be solidly asleep before he headed back to bed.

A hand slid across his shoulder and down his chest. Haven's eyes fell closed at Wren's touch. He took Wren's hand and brought it to his mouth, kissing it before coming to his feet. Hand in hand, they headed back to Wren's bedroom. As they cleared the door, Haven tugged Wren into his arms. He lifted Wren off his feet as their lips met and Wren's legs wrapped around his waist as their tongues stroked. With nothing between them but their pajama pants, there was no missing how hard Wren was for him. Haven's heart screamed for him to make love to Wren—slowly. Sweetly.

Haven took Wren to bed, gently bracing his fall as they went down on the mattress. He tugged at Wren's pants, peeling them down his thighs and savoring the sight of Wren's gorgeous body as it bared. With Wren nude and waiting, Haven pushed his pants down before grabbing the lube and a condom. Wren watched in silence as Haven rolled the sheath down his length and coated it with lube.

"You're so beautiful." The whispered praise caressed Haven's ears and squeezed his heart. Wren rarely gave compliments. Haven knew he meant it.

"And you're amazing," Haven said, settling between Wren's thighs. "I don't want anyone else." It was the closest thing Haven could say to the truth as he pushed his way inside and slowly rocked.

They kissed and stroked, moving slowly toward the same goal—mutual pleasure. It was obvious they were in no hurry. Being connected was more important than release. Haven just wanted to touch Wren every place he could reach. He didn't want to stop. His heart screamed for more.

Haven was in love with Wren and he was in love with Finch. He was in love with the idea of keeping them. This was a position he never expected to be in. His entire life, he had been controlling and possessive, and now he felt like he didn't care what he had to give up as long as he could keep this tiny family. Haven didn't care if Wren dated other men for pay. He knew it was just business. He would snap a neck if Dex tried to get sexual again, but everything else was fine as long as this family was his. As long as this man was his. He would fight to keep them and keep them safe. Haven had found his place. It was right here in Wren's bed and arms.

SEVEN

TOBY: *So, random as fuck offer on the shortest possible notice. Dex Wise wants to pay you 5K to do another demo in an hour. This time, at a different location. Thoughts?*

For much longer than necessary, Haven stared at the message. Something felt... off. While it wasn't unheard of for Haven to get offers from the same person to do more than one party, there was just something scratching at his skin with this one. The last party he had done for Dex hadn't gone well, so it didn't make sense for him to offer twice his fee for a second gig. Haven decided to dig a little deeper.

Haven: *Is it a longer drive or something?*

Toby: *Not really, no. It's at a ranch here in Austin. I THINK he's offering more money, and this is just conjecture on my part, because this one is on location at his latest filming spot. I wonder if he'll want you to sign a release so he can film bits to air. It's a reality show, so it's possible. If so, that could be huge for you. National spotlight. If nothing else, it might help boost your book sales.*

Fuck. Haven couldn't turn that down. He just wished he didn't feel so weird about it.

Haven: *Text me the address. I'll be there.*

The moment Haven sent the text, he regretted it. He didn't want to be in Dex's pocket. It was bad enough that Wren was so dependent on the guy. A thought occurred to him.

Haven: *Where are you?*

Wren: *On location with Dex. They're setting up to film in a few.*

Haven: *I'm on my way there. Dex just called in a special request for my demo for tonight. So, I guess I'll see you there.*

Wren: ***happy clapping** I'll shoot you longing looks from across the room.*

Haven: *I can't wait.*

He really couldn't. Haven just wished he didn't have such a bad feeling about this. The drive to the Crooked Creek Ranch was nice. It was quiet back roads with very little traffic. Haven supposed the location cut down on background noise while filming a reality show. He forced his mind to stick to mundane things. Otherwise, he might think about Dex and Wren and Dex being with Wren. Haven wasn't bothered by that, which was insane when he thought about it. But really, Wren and Haven had a healthy, grown up, and even-footed relationship. They just clicked and never felt out of balance. Haven didn't know how to explain it. He just felt normal.

For once, Haven was completely happy with exactly where he was in life, and... goddamn it. That was precisely why this job bugged him so much. Things were going too well. He had finally found what he had been searching for and karma still owed him a few hits. The only thing he had worth taking was Wren and Finch. Maybe one of these days, he would stop feeling like he would probably lose them any second. Today wasn't that day. Today, he felt like Dex Wise was about to rip away everything he loved, and Haven had no clue how to stop it.

HANGING OUT WITH DEX WAS ACTUALLY A BIT boring some days. Today was one of those days. Dex was too busy to chat, but for whatever reason, he wanted Wren underfoot. Wren couldn't complain. The money was always good.

"Why does Dex call you fire sprite?"

A smile tugged at the corners of Wren's mouth. Colt was fearless. Wren would give him that. He turned and smiled up at Colt. "Because calling me a demon wouldn't be cute. How have you been?"

Colt had dimples. It was adorable. A slight blush tinged his cheeks, making his blue eyes seem even bluer. "I Googled that Cubs for Rent place. Do people actually pay you for absolutely nothing but to go to dinner or whatever? That seems insane."

Damn. Colt was a funny guy. Wren chuckled. "Yep. People actually pay to do things with me. I know. Scandalous."

"Oh, no," Colt said, sounding horrified. "I can one hundred percent see people paying to be seen with you, but can just anyone be doing this? Like, can I really charge people to take me out on a date?"

"Of course." Wren could see people searching for a sexy cowboy. "Here." Wren dug out his wallet and found a Cubs for Rent card. "Call the number and tell whoever answers that Wren sent you their way and you're interested in listing yourself on their site. They'll walk you through everything and take care of scheduling. All you have to do is show up where you're told to show up, wearing the appropriate attire for what you've been hired to do. No one is allowed to touch you or anything like that. If you end up doing anything with anyone, just make sure they understand very clearly that you're off the clock and you chose them willingly. You don't want any misunderstandings."

Colt accepted the card and looked it over thoughtfully. "I don't know if I'll call, but that's pretty cool. Do you make a lot of money at this? Not trying to be rude."

It took a lot to insult Wren. He shrugged. "In my case—"

"He makes a fuck ton of money. Move along," Dex said, appearing out of nowhere. He looked angry as he inserted himself between them. "Come, pet. We have plans."

Wren winked at Colt and allowed himself to get pulled away. Even though he wasn't sure why Dex didn't want him talking to Colt, Dex was paying his fee. Dex linked fingers with him and led him inside the house where the contestants stayed. It was huge and dirty. Honestly, Wren was scared to touch anything. The place smelled like liquor and he was pretty sure there was a cum stain on the couch. A few people were looking at him with open hostility, which Wren didn't understand at all. Wren pasted on his most flirtatious persona like a protective armor and clung to Dex's arm like a harlot. If people wanted to see him as competition, he would be better than they ever hoped to be. Wren knew how to earn jealousy.

"I don't know if I want to sit on this furniture," Wren whispered for Dex's ears.

Dex tossed a laughing glance his way. "Be not afraid, fire sprite. You're sitting in my lap tonight." That was all the warning Wren got before Dex plopped down in a cushy chair and pulled Wren into his lap.

With a shrug, Wren turned sideways and settled in. At least he knew Dex was clean. Before Wren could ask what was going on, the door opened again, and Haven stepped inside. He was in the company of some guy who worked for the show. His gaze slid Wren's way for half a second before he went back to listening to whatever instructions were being handed out. The college brats were eyeing Haven like their next meal. Wren bit back a grin. That meal was his. Wren couldn't wait to have him alone.

Dex touched his lips to the shell of Wren's ear. "I didn't get to watch this the last time I hired this guy."

His fingers brushed down Wren's spine. "I'm intrigued."

Wren was too. He chewed his bottom lip and stared at Haven with all the longing in his heart. Haven's gaze kept sliding his way before quickly moving away—like he had to force himself to look at other people. Wren barely heard a word being said. He couldn't stop reading Haven's every gesture, searching for his thoughts. Wren didn't know if Haven felt anything for him besides lust. In truth, Wren wasn't sure if he wanted Haven to love him back. That was a lie. He was dying for Haven to feel the same. Maybe they had no chance at making things real. It was more than possible that Wren was setting himself up for heartbreak. He didn't know what he was doing anymore.

"Who wants to volunteer?"

Wren might not have heard the question if Haven hadn't looked so wicked asking it.

"Dex's man looks like he likes a steady hand with a belt. Maybe he should do it."

Wren fought the urge to hiss at the catty brown-haired bitch who spoke up. The problem was, he really wanted to volunteer for whatever Haven needed.

Dex's arm tightened around Wren's middle.

"Wren is just fine where he is. I say Colt could use a little rope burn in his life."

Colt flashed an irritated glance Dex's way at the comment, but he defiantly stood as the room broke into a round of agreement. It seemed he was a hardass on the show and everyone relished the idea of seeing him tied and humiliated. Haven kept his gaze locked on the rope he readied for demo—like it was his sanity. Something felt... wrong.

Dex lightly kissed his neck. "Relax. No one is tying you up. I'll make that little girl wish she'd never met me, though. She's been a problem from day one."

Wren flashed Dex a smile he didn't feel. He appreciated Dex's willingness to destroy someone on his behalf. It was just that something wasn't right with Haven. His refusal to look Wren's way was starting to feel choking rather than adorable. While Haven still wore an engaging and naughty expression, drawing people in, there was a brittle edge to him. Wren probably wouldn't have noticed if he didn't know Haven so well. The rest of the demonstration felt like it dragged on forever. By the time Haven was packing up to leave, Wren was ready to leap from Dex's lap and into Haven's arms just to get Haven to look at him.

Dex's fingers encircled Wren's throat. His lips

brushed the shell of Wren's ear as Haven headed out. Wren's eyes followed him every step of the way. "You should probably go home now, fire sprite. You're off the clock. Unless you want to stay," he added, stroking Wren's neck.

The wave of relief was intense. "You're right. I should go. Finch will probably call at the crack of dawn since tomorrow is our usual day to go to the park."

Another light kiss caressed his ear before Dex released him. "Be careful going to your car."

Wren kissed his cheek and stood. He tried to measure his steps while his brain screamed for him to run. Wren wanted to catch Haven before he got away. The moment he was outside and out of sight, Wren nearly sprinted toward the designated parking area. It was a bean field that Wren always prayed didn't swallow his car. He spotted Haven's tall form cutting through the cars.

"Hold up, Haven. Let's go do something."

Haven slowed and turned at Wren's yelled words. "You should go back inside."

Wren's brow furrowed at the odd statement. "I don't want to go back inside. My time here is up. Plus, you're the one I want to spend my time with."

For a long, drawn-out moment, Haven stared at

Wren in silence. When he finally spoke, his response only confused Wren more. "I got someone killed once."

Wren blinked. "Okay." Even he heard the confusion in his response, but Wren didn't know what else he was supposed to say to that pronouncement.

Haven scrubbed his hand through his hair, looking ready to fall apart. When he met Wren's gaze again, Wren almost took a step back at the intensity of his stare. "You remind me of him. He had an owner too."

A shot of outrage punched Wren in the chest. "*Nobody* owns me."

A humorless laugh escaped Haven. He shook his head—like he couldn't believe Wren's stupidity. "I knew something was up with Dex hiring me tonight, but I couldn't put my finger on it." He shook his head again. A self-deprecating smile hovered on his lips. "It just felt wrong, you know. But I get it now. Dex needed me to see it. He wanted to sit as close as possible and look me in the eye with you in his lap so I would understand that you are his."

Wren scoffed. "I don't belong to Dex. He's a client. I thought you understood this is my job. This is the only way I can support Finch."

Haven pulled a pained face. His voice cracked when he spoke. "Oh, I know. I get that Dex is the reason you have custody and the reason you're not homeless and Finch gets the care he deserves. I want all those things for you, but also, I want you alive and he needed me to see that he is the one who controls all of those things."

Wren's chest hurt. Haven was saying all these things and they didn't make sense. They wouldn't stick to his brain in a way that formed a picture he could relate to his life. "I don't understand."

"Baby, I'm not a BDSM master. I'm just some controlling asshole who likes tying men to the bed. I'm also the reason a nineteen-year-old boy will forever be nineteen, because I didn't heed the warnings when I saw he belonged to someone else. Tonight wasn't about a demo. This was Dex telling me you are his. I can't afford to ignore that warning twice in my life. Finch needs you more than I do. I can't let you get hurt because of me. I can't live with knowing you're no longer in the world because I had to beat my chest and challenge Dex. Your life is more important than my heart. I love you, Wren. It matters to me that you're somewhere in the world, cooking Finch's favorite foods and taking him to the park. I love you enough to love from a distance, because if I don't, Dex will rip away everything he's given you and he wanted me to see him and know it."

Other than Finch, no one had ever told Wren they loved him that he could recall. This was definitely the first time anyone had used the words like a weapon, ripping out his heart. Wren wanted to say something, anything at all. Pain kept his tongue glued to the roof of his mouth. Years of refusing to be weak froze him now. Haven looked wrecked—like he fully believed everything he said. For a full minute, Wren struggled to don his usual carefree mask so Haven could walk away without guilt. He couldn't do it, so Wren walked away without a word or looking back.

Wren didn't pay attention to where he was headed. He walked for several minutes before the fog in his brain lifted enough to let him take in his surroundings. Fuck. His car was in the opposite direction. Wren stood still and tried to plan his next move. His heart hurt too bad to think straight. He had let Haven in. Now he didn't know how to shove him out. Wren spotted a circle of lawn chairs around scorched ground—like someone had enjoyed a bonfire recently. He headed toward them and sat in the closest chair.

For a long time, Wren stared at the night sky,

seeing nothing. The air cooled. How would he tell Finch that Haven was gone? A sharp pain slashed across his heart. His eyes and nose burned. Finch would be so brokenhearted. All people did was break their hearts. He had known better. Wren had been so stupid. He hurt too badly to decipher the exact moment he had gone wrong. It was his fault, though. That much Wren knew without a doubt. Everything was always his fault.

"I thought you went home." Wren startled at the appearance of Colt, settling into the chair beside him.

Wren looked his way and forced his tongue to work. "No. Not yet."

Colt took off his cowboy hat and set it on his knee. He was blond. Wren had never noticed. He had nice hair. Colt ran his fingers through it, sweeping it back. It looked soft. "So, that was a hell of a show, wasn't it?"

A hint of a smile touched Wren's lips. He didn't feel it in his heart. "Was that your first time being tied up?" Wren squeezed his hands together and twisted his fingers, physically trying to hold his shit together.

"That's not what I meant. That was a hell of a

show Dex put on for your man. Did it work, scaring him away?"

Wren's gaze moved Colt's way. His heart beat loudly in his ears. "How is everyone seeing this but me?"

A sexy smile touched Colt's lips. "In my profession, you only meet three types of people. Bum buckle chasers. Poor cow pokes," he said, motioning toward himself. "and rich ranchers who've never been told no in their lives. Now, meeting Dex and all the people he's brought out here has proven to me that the whole world is the same. People chasing dreams. People killing their souls for every dime," he said, motioning Wren's way. "and people like Dex who've never been told no in their whole lives."

"Actually, Dex falls in all three categories because he was poor growing up, and wait..." It hit Wren. "How did you know Mister Haven was my man?"

"Was? I guess he got his way," Colt said, sounding as if it was meant more for him than Wren. He took a breath. "Dex made an announcement earlier that he had hired your man to come in and do a demo he thought would make for fun clips for the show."

Wren stood so fast, he knocked his chair over. No one knew Haven was his. Even Wren hadn't fully accepted it until he had gotten dumped. There was no way Dex should know. "Excuse me. I have to go." Wren walked away without looking back. A haze of fury coated his vision. By the time he reached Dex's trailer, he was ready to rip Dex's limbs from his body. He threw the door open without bothering to knock.

Dex looked up from the script he held. He eyed Wren for a moment before speaking. "Angry looks good on you, fire sprite. Did you forget something?"

"Is it true?"

Dex set aside the script and gave Wren his full attention. "You'll have to be more specific."

Wren took a breath, hoping to stop himself from scratching Dex's eyes out. When he spoke, his voice sounded calm but scary. "Did you invite Haven here so you could warn him away?"

"No."

Confusion rendered Wren mute. Dex was a lot of things, but a liar wasn't one. He didn't need to lie. Lying inferred caring to an extent. Dex cared about nothing.

A loud sigh escaped Dex. He stood and closed the distance between them. Wren found himself being led to the couch with no input from his brain.

He had no idea what happened to his life in the past few hours. Wren was numb.

"Look," Dex said, settling in next to him. "Did I invite... Did you say his name is Haven?"

Wren nodded, still trying to rub two thoughts together.

"Did I invite Haven here to get under his skin? Yes, *but*," Dex said, speaking loudly before Wren could jump in. "I did not do it to come between you two. I did it because I care."

Wren's brow furrowed. "But you don't care about anyone."

Dex snorted. It was an ugly sound. "You're so blind, fire spite. Or maybe I should say, you only see what you want to see. How could you think I don't care? Think about it. No one else gets dates with you, if I can help it. I've made sure Finch is taken care of, and you got custody, while finding a way to get you out of that damn strip club. No one has shown you more love than I have, and—before you get it in your head—my doing those things doesn't have a damn thing to do with you sharing my bed. I can get anyone to share my bed. What I can't do is find anyone to put up with me long enough to genuinely care about me, and if I know nothing else, I know you care." Dex looked real for the first time ever. "You're my best friend, Wren. I want you to be safe and happy. If this guy makes you happy, then I have no plans to stand in the way of that." Dex's voice hardened. "But I will fucking slit his throat and burn his body if he hurts you, and he's not allowed to take you away from me. I won't let anyone put you in the position of being completely dependent on them —love or not. You've fought too hard to keep Finch safe and healthy. He's your family and he needs you. I need you too. So if this guy wants to be with you, then he gets me too. I needed him to see that."

Wren didn't know how to feel. Mostly, he was just sad. "I don't know much about having friends, but I'm pretty sure you could've just said all that instead of ruining my relationship. Haven was totally fine with this," he said, motioning between them. "until you made it look like I'm your personal property. You... I can't... I don't even know what to say." He stood. "But I think I'm done." He headed for the door.

Dex jumped up and blocked his path. "It wasn't my intention to ruin anything, fire sprite. Don't leave upset. I'll talk to Haven and explain that I'm not good at making points sometimes."

"Oh, you made your point," Wren yelled. His temper completely snapped. "He sees me now."

Wren's eyes filled with tears. He swiped them away, refusing to show weakness. "You made sure he saw exactly what I've become so I can cling to the one family member I have left. He knows I sold my soul." Wren swallowed, trying to breathe. When he spoke again, he couldn't make his voice go above a whisper. "I've always known you own me, but—before tonight —I never regretted the decision to entrust my life to you, because I thought—despite all signs to the contrary—you were a good man. It breaks my heart to realize how wrong I was about you, because you were my best friend too. Now I don't ever want to see your face again." While Dex still looked like Wren slapped him, Wren stole his chance and stepped around him. He didn't look back after making it out the door. His feet didn't stop moving for anything until he reached his car. If Dex came after him, Wren was too angry to hear it. He had lost too much today. His heart couldn't take another second of being here.

EIGHT

IT DIDN'T ESCAPE Wren's notice that the weather matched his mood. Rain fell in drowning sheets, casting the day into gray shadows. Wren pressed his forehead to his screen door and watched the shower drench the earth. It wasn't supposed to last long, but he still wouldn't be able to take Finch to the park after this. The ground would be too muddy.

I love you, Wren. Those words played through Wren's mind like a soundtrack set on repeat. Was this horrible feeling in his chest really what people searched for all their lives? He had to say, it kind of sucked. Damn. Haven had looked so beautiful saying those words—like he meant them. They were only words, though. Words without actions were just excuses. The thing Wren wanted most from Haven was Haven. He needed Haven. Otherwise, Wren was just swimming upstream, fighting for air while delaying the inevitable. *I love you, Wren.* It was crazy. He had never expected anyone to love him.

Wren moved to the couch. He needed to leave and go see Finch. First, Wren had to find a way to kill the pain. Finch was too good at sensing Wren's mood. He wasn't ready to talk about losing Haven. Wren's phone buzzed, pulling him from the hole he drowned himself in.

Finch: *It's raining. Can Haven come play with me?*

Wren clasped the phone between his hands, set his elbows on his knees, and beat his head on his hands. Jesus. He didn't know how to handle this one. Wren didn't want to lie to Finch or give him hope that Haven would come around again. But neither did he want to break Finch's heart. Fuck. With a deep breath for strength, Wren started typing and dodging.

Wren: *I'm not sure what Haven is doing today, sweetie. I haven't heard from him. If you want, I can come play games with you instead.*

Finch: *You give up too easy. It's okay. I'll call Haven and ask him.*

For a full thirty seconds, Wren blinked at his

phone. He didn't remember Haven giving Finch his number. Wren didn't know what to say. His gut reaction was to tell Finch not to bother. He was too damn shocked to react.

Finch: *Haven says it's okay with him if it's okay with you. So, is it okay?*

Well, goddamn. This was a conundrum.

Wren: *That's fine with me, but I'm not sure if the nurses will let him in without me there.*

Finch: *I want you to come too. I just don't want to play with you.*

A chuckle escaped Wren as he read Finch's text. Finch kept a check on Wren's ego, for sure. Wren's smile slipped away. It looked like he would be spending the day with Haven. Fantastic. It was like he was living a nightmare sometimes.

Wren: *I'll be there soon. I love you.*

Finch: *I love you too. See you soon.*

Wren prayed he could do this, because what choice did he have? Finch had fallen in love with Haven. It was Wren's fault for bringing him around. Now Wren had to get cozy in the bed he had made. He had a lot to figure out—like how to break his brother's heart. Jesus. He was a terrible person.

Haven hadn't slept all night. Everything hurt, including his heart. He needed to grab his assignments from Toby and hit the road so he could spend a few hours with Finch. No one had been more surprised than him when Finch called. He hadn't known what to say. Haven didn't have the heart to tell him they probably couldn't hang out any longer. Goddamn. Haven couldn't breathe. He wished Toby would hurry up so he could stop staring at the inside of their gorgeous house. He hated rich people today.

"How is operation changing your stripes going?" Tucker asked, appearing from nowhere and sounding like he knew it was going beautifully.

The joke was on the jokester for once, because Haven's life was complete shit. "Well, I guess it depends on your definition of success. I haven't been the least bit controlling since Wren and I started dating, if you don't account for me telling him he's Dex Wise's property so I won't be seeing him anymore."

Tucker's eyebrows hit his hairline.

"Speaking of Dex, he's booked you again," Toby said, strolling into the room with his gaze locked on Haven's schedule.

Tucker hadn't stopped blinking or staring at

Haven in shocked silence yet—like Haven broke his brain.

Haven focused on Toby. "I'm not interested in doing another show for Dex."

"That's too bad," Toby said, lifting his gaze. "I already agreed on your behalf. You have two hours until you're scheduled to be there. Apparently, this is really important to him and no isn't an option."

Haven's temper spiked. "It'll do Dex some good to not get his way for once. I'm not interested."

Toby didn't look the least bit put off by Haven's anger. "He's offering twenty-five thousand for one hour, and he's an important client." That last part was said in the tone of a man who still considered Haven on thin ice. Haven spent a moment considering how much he wanted their friendship and this job. He didn't really need it, but it made his life much easier. His book royalties paid the bare minimum of his bills, with nothing left over. It was also a lot less stressful marketing his books if he didn't completely depend on them for survival. But was the extra money worth his soul? He didn't know. In the end, it had nothing to do with money. Haven knew he could walk away from this gig guilt free, except he couldn't do that if he damaged Cubs for Rent's reputation. Haven didn't doubt for a second

Dex would destroy the Kodiak brothers if Haven disobeyed.

He took a steadying breath. "Same address as last night or as the first party?"

Tucker finally broke. "No. Haven. You can say no."

Haven refused to back down now. "It's fine. Life hasn't killed me yet. One more day of watching Dex flaunt Wren in my face is nothing, but after this demo, I'm done."

Toby seemed to slowly catch on that there was more to the story. "Wait. What did I miss?"

Haven's phone buzzed. He checked the face. There was a message from Finch. Fuck. He had gotten so angry about Dex, Haven had forgotten his plans with Finch.

Finch: *How much longer until you get here?*

Haven turned and took two steps toward the door before it occurred to him that his mind was made up already. "On second thought, tell Dex and his twenty-five grand they can suck my dick. I have a date with an adorable twelve-year-old. Find someone else to serve the spoiled masses."

"What did I miss?" Toby asked again, but Haven didn't look back. He was done with this shit. Maybe he had to live without his heart, but Haven would keep his pride. Dex couldn't have that too. Haven had plans with Finch. There wasn't enough money in the world that could make him break that kid's heart.

WREN MADE THE DRIVE TO TOBY'S WITH HIS heart in his throat. The minute he had gotten in his car to go see Finch, Toby had called him in for a meeting. Since he needed his job, he had called the home and given his permission for Haven to visit Finch before letting Finch know he would be late. Wren couldn't afford to blow off Toby right now. He had already walked away from every other source of income he had. While his savings account was in good shape right now, things would change when Finch moved home. Finch would still need part time care. Wren would have to hire someone to stay with Finch while he worked, and that wouldn't be cheap. It wasn't like he could hire some teenage babysitter.

Panic seized Wren, the way it did sometimes when he wasn't expecting it. What if he couldn't do this? He couldn't trust just anyone to stay with Finch. Fuck. Wren was only twenty. He had no business being responsible for someone else's life. Wren took a breath. It didn't help. His vision darkened around the edges. Toby's house came into view and Wren quickly pulled into the driveway and put the car in park. Each breath he took came harder than the last. No oxygen made it to his brain. He tried breathing harder and faster, trying not to drown on dry land. There was no air. His car door flew open and a voice screamed in his ear. Nothing penetrated his panic. He was going to die, and Finch would be all alone. Wren couldn't stop it from happening. No matter how hard he tried to breathe, he couldn't get his lungs to inflate.

"For fuck's sake. Put your head between your knees."

Wren found himself turned sideways, hanging half out of the car and bent at the waist. His hearing slowly returned. The first sound that reached him was wheezing. It took a second for Wren to realize the noise came from him. Then a voice cut through his fear.

"That's it. You're okay. Just breathe."

"I see what you're saying. They're definitely dating. I would recognize that soul-sucking panic anywhere."

"I don't think they're dating anymore," someone

else said, making Wren realize he had a huge audience.

He tried to lift his head, but his body still wasn't working right.

"Just give yourself a minute."

Wren finally managed to lift his head enough to focus on the person soothing him. It was Jericho. Fantastic. It was Wren's greatest dream to fall apart in front of the guy who had married Haven's ex.

"I need everyone to get lost. This isn't a show," Loyal said, wheeling into the middle of everything.

"This is my job," Jericho argued. "He needs medical attention."

Wren sat up and blinked at the crowd he had attracted. Loyal, Toby, Jericho, and some guy he had never seen before surrounded him.

Loyal waved off Jericho's words. "He needs everyone to stop looking at him. Go on," he said, shooing everyone away. "I've got this." Even though no one looked happy to be leaving Loyal and Wren alone, they grumbled their way to the house. Loyal waited until they were alone before focusing on Wren again. He gave his lap a pat. "Would you like a lift inside?"

Despite the situation, Wren bit back a smile. Loyal hadn't asked what was wrong, and Wren appreciated that more than the guy would ever know. "I'm pretty sure I can walk."

"The offer stands."

Wren nodded but didn't move. He sat, staring at Loyal instead. He took note of the man's blond hair and bluish-green eyes. Loyal was heart-stopping and it was impossible to miss. Yet Wren didn't think he had ever noticed. When he thought about it, Wren realized he didn't really look at people. He saw them and sometimes took note of their features, but he never really felt moved by anyone's looks.

"You're very beautiful."

Loyal looked taken aback by Wren's matter-of-fact claim. "Um. Thank you. You are too."

"No. Not really," Wren said, sounding tired even to his ears. "I'm actually pretty plain. It's always been strange to me that anyone would pay to spend time with me or watch me dance in a thong. I'm not really special in any way at all." Wren finally managed to push to his feet. He closed his car door and motioned toward the house. "After you."

Loyal didn't move. "Are you sure you're okay?"

Wren dug deep and found his armor. He smiled. "Yes. I'm good." It didn't matter if it was true. This was the life Wren had been given. He had no choice but to live it.

With a nod, Loyal headed for the house. Wren followed while doing his best to pack everything away. Loyal led him inside and down the hall until they ended up inside a large office. Thankfully, only Toby waited inside. Wren wasn't up for giving everyone another show.

Toby glanced up from his spot behind the desk as they cleared the door. He lit from the inside out at the first sight of Loyal. Wren's chest hurt. He shoved the pain aside. Beautiful people deserved to be loved. Wren would never be beautiful. He was too tainted on the inside, where it mattered.

The moment Wren sat across from Toby; Toby jumped in with both feet. "Sorry for the short notice. We've been forced to do a bit of scrambling today. Mister had like six parties booked for this afternoon and tonight, and he quit." Wren blinked at the news. Toby didn't give him time to question anything. "Luckily, Kevin gave us a few names of some other BDSM masters, and we were able to cover his bookings, but unless one of those people wants the job permanently, we probably can't offer that service any longer." Toby pulled a face. "You have no idea how much we appreciate the fact that you always show up where you're hired to be. Nobody likes being stood up. It's doubly bad when they've paid their date to be there."

"I can't afford to no-show," Wren said, being honest. He had some other truths to dole out while he was at it. "With that said, I—"

"We'd like to offer you a new position," Loyal said, cutting him off. "A salary spot, plus commission."

Wren blinked. "Um. Okay."

Toby nodded. "You're our best and most requested escort. Plus, people genuinely like you. We think, if someone gets stood up by an escort on our site, they would be more than satisfied if they got you as a backup. So we would like to offer you a flat salary to be on standby. This would take the place of you having regular clients. Instead, if we have a client who has a no-show escort, we would send you instead. You get the no-show escort's fee as extra commission on top of your salary. We would make sure your pay was worth giving up your current client list, of course."

Wren's gaze moved from Toby to Loyal and back again. They looked hopeful—like they weren't completely saving Wren right when he thought Dex would most likely destroy him financially. There was still one problem. "This sounds amazing, but I recently got full custody of Finch and I don't know how hard it'll be to find someone to keep him at a moment's notice like that. This position would be a lifesaver, though. Can I think about it? Obviously, I'm interested." Especially since they had just watched him break down and still offered him this job. "I just need to figure out how to handle Finch and working, you know." He took a breath as he heard the panic rising in his voice again.

"He could stay here with us, if it comes down to it," Loyal offered, taking Wren by surprise. "I mean, he's an awesome kid and our house is wheelchair friendly, obviously. If he feels comfortable coming here, we don't mind having him as a last-minute guest, if you need the help."

These people were too good to be true. "Are you sure? He adores everyone here, but he's not independent. Finch needs a lot of help with a lot of things."

Loyal's smile never dimmed. "So do I. We can help each other. Not to mention, Toby is like hero material and my dad is a fireman. He has lots of medical training. This is the perfect place for him to hang out if you get a call."

Wren wasn't a crier. Not really. Life had been too hard and kicked most of the tears out of him years ago. But he truly thought he might cry then. He had to clear his throat to speak. "In that case, this new position sounds amazing." To his horror, a tear slid down his cheek. Wren wiped it away and quickly stood. "If that's all, I have plans with Finch today."

Toby and Loyal exchanged a glance. Toby was the one who spoke first. "You know you're not alone, right?"

Wren froze. He hurt so goddamn bad, he didn't know where to go with it. Haven had said he loved Wren and then dumped him. Dex had said Wren was his best friend while ripping away Wren's perception of reality. No one's actions matched their words anymore. Wren couldn't trust anyone but himself. That was one lesson life kept teaching him every day.

"That's not the least bit true. If you want, we can talk later tonight or tomorrow at length about this new position. Right now, I have to honor my plans with my brother."

Loyal looked crestfallen.

Toby seemed resigned. He nodded. "I understand. Family always comes first."

With a nod, Wren turned to leave. Before he made it five steps, Loyal spoke up, stopping him. "Just so you know, Mister quit because he decided he would rather spend his time with Finch. I know it feels like no one has your back, but—no matter what's happened—Mister loves your brother and you, from what I hear."

Wren didn't bother to comment. There was no need to point out that loving someone wasn't enough. Their lives were different. They had money and each other. These men had a family and house filled with love. They didn't understand doing the unthinkable to survive. Wren had himself. That was who he could depend on to be there at the end of the day. He wouldn't forget that again.

NINE

AFTER TWO HOURS OF GAMING, Haven had to step out to save Finch's pride while a nurse came in to care for him. He didn't know how long this routine lasted, but Haven knew he needed some air. It was a lot harder than he ever imagined, spending the whole day wondering if this would be the last time he saw Finch. He wondered if Wren would let him keep visiting. It wouldn't be long before Finch moved home, and then Wren really wouldn't want him coming around. Here, Wren could avoid him. That wouldn't be the case much longer.

The second Haven stepped outside; he saw red. Dex was leaned against the hood of Haven's car—like a man prepared to wait all day. Haven almost went back inside. It would serve Dex right if Haven left him waiting the rest of the day. He was too angry to go that route. It was one thing to warn him away from Wren, but it seemed he wouldn't be allowed to visit Finch either. Finch was a kid. He didn't deserve this meddling.

Haven's angry stride ate up the distance between them. Dex didn't look the least bit fazed by Haven's open hostility. Before Haven could jump into the man with both feet, Dex beat him to the punch.

"What a disappointment you've turned out to be."

Haven drew up short at the insult. "What do you want, Dex? I already told Toby I wasn't interested in being bought."

"That's dumb as hell, if I do say so myself. Twenty-five thousand is nothing to me. That's like a tip at dinner. I could spend ten times that every single day for the rest of my life and still die a billionaire. You should've taken the money." He straightened away from Haven's car. "But that's not why I'm here. You were supposed to be up to the challenge. I really thought you loved Wren. People disappoint me daily, but I'm not usually this wrong when it comes to reading people. I truly expected better of you."

Between not sleeping and the pain crushing his heart, Haven didn't have the patience to play games. "As much as this may shock you, I don't live to please you. So whatever it was you expected of me, I don't give a fuck. What do you want? I'm trying to spend some time with the kid."

Dex smirked. His blue eyes glowed with humor at Haven's expense. "Now, see, there's something you're getting right. So tell me why you're such a pussy when it comes to Wren. I mean, he's sexy and likable. He's definitely kinky enough for someone like you. Yet, at the first hint of a challenge, you walked away. Why is that?"

Haven had never been more confused in his life. Yesterday, Dex had been issuing a silent warning to stay away from Wren. Now he was calling Haven to the carpet for staying away from Wren. Wasn't he? Hell, Haven didn't know anymore.

"Is there a point to this conversation? You made it clear yesterday that Wren belongs to you. I get it. You're funding all of this," he said, waving dismissively at the building. "And I'm nobody. What do you want from me?"

Dex's eyebrows rose. "I want you to be the man I thought you were and love Wren the way he deserves."

"But…" Haven had nothing. Dex had clearly been flexing his money and power yesterday. Now, today it was because he wanted Haven in Wren's life. What the actual fuck?

"Look," Dex said, shoving his hands in his pockets. "You could have been listening to all this while making twenty-five grand, but you made me break my usual set schedule and drive all the way over here, which I fucking hate, so now you're going to listen to it for free. All this," he said, waving toward the building. "has been here long before you came around. It'll be here long after you're gone. Maybe I'm just some guy with a checkbook, but I've been writing those checks a long time. While you've spent the last few years pining after your ex, Wren has been struggling and doing whatever it took to survive. If you're really not planning to stick around, then get lost. I'm not going anywhere. Even if he hates me now because of you, I'll keep writing those checks. But if you don't plan to stick around, then you don't have a single goddamn reason to be here now. You've got nothing to offer but yourself. If you're telling me now that's not worth keeping because you run at the first sign of competition, then get in your car and go. Wren needs me, because he can't do this alone. He needs you for the same reason. But, like it or not, he does need us both. You stepped into a huge package deal when you kept showing up at that strip club, so what's it going to be?"

It dawned on Haven. Dex's threat was no real threat at all. "Wait." Haven's forehead furrowed. "That whole show yesterday, that was just to warn me you planned to keep hiring Wren?" Haven blinked some more, trying to wrap his mind around the situation. "Well, that's just... dumb as fuck," Haven said, finally finding the words he had been searching for. "I know you're a part of Wren's life. For fuck's sake, I met him in your driveway. Maybe you expect people to change and bend to your ideal, but I fell in love with Wren exactly as he is. I don't want him to change. Not to mention, he has all of this responsibility on his shoulders. I knew about everything going in. Plus, seriously? At any point in time, you could have called me up and been like, hey man. I care about Wren and want to be a part of his life. I would absolutely back that, because I know you were there for him back when no one else was and you kept showing up even when he had other options." The longer Haven ranted, the more Dex changed until he looked like a different person. Approachable. That fact kept Haven bitching. "Jesus Christ. You obviously had me investigated, which means you should've been able to figure out I was more concerned for Wren's safety if I kept seeing him than I ever was about what you could do to me. I've got nothing to take, but Wren and Finch, so— next time—why don't you just try using your goddamn words."

"Fair enough." A huge smile exploded across Dex's face. "I knew you had some fire in there."

A burble of laughter gathered in Haven's throat. He had no idea why the situation suddenly struck him as funny, but he couldn't stop the roar of laughter from bursting out. Haven swiped at his eyes and took a breath. "So... You've known Wren the longest. How do we convince him to forgive us?"

Dex's smile slipped away. "That's a good question. Wren is likely to do just about anything to ensure he never needs either of us again. He let himself be vulnerable, and now." Dex shrugged.

That was exactly what Haven was afraid of the most. Wren had dropped his guard just long enough for Haven to sucker punch him. Now he might never let anyone else near the real him again. A car door slammed. Dex and Haven turned at the sound.

Wren walked their way with his head down. He glanced up, catching sight of them. His step slowed as his gaze moved between them. Without a word or another look their way, Wren headed for the building. His closed expression gave nothing away.

Dex slapped Haven across the back. "Good luck. You won him once when no one else has. You can do it again. I'm counting on you. If he can't forgive you, he damn sure won't forgive me. Go take one for the team."

Great. Haven hadn't groveled in a while. If anyone was worth it, it was Wren. He would try until he couldn't try anymore. God knew he had nothing else.

THEY WERE TOGETHER. WHY IN THE HELL WERE Dex and Haven together? Wren's nerves couldn't be stretched further. He was half a second away from a complete breakdown. The only relief was being with Finch. Wren paused outside his door, took a deep breath, and tapped lightly on the door before he stepped inside.

Finch was in bed. He flashed Wren a huge smile that looked like pure joy. Wren had to blink back tears. Finch was his only happiness. He was a pure soul in an ugly world.

"Hey, sweetie. Are you tired?"

Finch gave him an awkward and jerky nod. "I got up early to go to the park."

Wren took a shaky breath. "Yeah. I'm so sorry about that. Maybe we can find something indoors to do tomorrow. Did you have fun gaming with Haven?" Damn. Even saying Haven's name hurt.

"He's coming back, but I'm..." Finch obviously lost his voice mid-speech.

Wren filled the chair beside his bed and rubbed his arm. "It's okay. Close your eyes." Haven slipped back inside the room. Wren's gaze moved Haven's way as he tried easing Finch. "I'm sure Haven doesn't mind waiting to finish your game on another day."

Haven flashed a smile Finch's way. "Absolutely. I'm good to come back whenever you want."

Wren swallowed hard at Haven's claim. Everything hurt. Why did he have to meet this guy—this person who was everything Wren needed and wanted? It was cruel to know Haven existed and they wouldn't be together. *Mister quit because he would rather spend his time with Finch.* Those words were a knife in Wren's heart. Wren dropped his gaze to his lap and continued rubbing Finch's arm. He no longer knew if he comforted Finch or himself. Wren was so damn weary. Haven's hands landed on his shoulders. He massaged, making Wren's eyes fall closed. His throat swelled. He was so in love with this man who didn't want to be part of his life anymore. It wasn't fair. A tear escaped him. Wren tried wiping it away on the sly. He sniffed as quietly as possible, hoping not to give himself away.

"Haven?" Finch sounded so tired and small.

"What do you need, buddy?"

"Wren is crying."

Fuck. This was some bullshit. "I'm fine." He would be fine even if it killed him.

"That's my fault," Haven said, taking Wren by surprise. "Sometimes I say dumb things that I don't mean."

Tears flowed freely now. It had been so long since Wren shed more than a tear or two at a time, it was like a dam broke.

"You should say you're sorry."

Haven squeezed Wren's shoulders at Finch's suggestion. "I plan to, because I love you both, and I would never want to make either of you cry."

"Haven?"

Wren bit back a smile at Finch's half-asleep voice. He was fighting hard against sleep today.

"Yeah?" Haven said the word so quietly, it was obvious he was testing to make sure Finch hadn't fallen asleep.

"You should marry Wren before someone else does."

A soft and sexy-sounding chuckle rumbled behind Wren. "That's my plan."

Wren's head whipped around so fast, he almost hurt himself. Haven looked completely sincere. He held Wren's stare without blinking.

"I love you," Haven mouthed.

Wren didn't know how to feel. Mostly, he hurt. Haven gave him whiplash with his back and forth. He didn't know if he could trust Haven again. Maybe he was nothing more than false words.

Haven touched his lips to the shell of Wren's ear. "He's out. Come outside with me."

Wren didn't know why he let Haven take his hand and lead him out the door. It seemed like he should pull his hand away and leave Haven in the dust. Instead, he held tight.

Haven dug out his keys and unlocked his car with the keyfob before opening the passenger side door for Wren. With a breath for strength, Wren climbed inside. He had already lost Haven. There wasn't much else the man could do to him now.

Haven circled the car and climbed behind the wheel, except he didn't stop there after closing the door. He kept coming until his mouth covered Wren's. Wren didn't have the strength to push him away.

"I'm sorry. I'm so, so sorry," Haven said between kisses. "Last night, I just misread the situation and overreacted. You deserve better. I'm so sorry."

Wren's heart squeezed. He didn't want to give up Haven's lips, but Wren couldn't let Haven take the blame. "No. You were right. Dex admitted he invited you there to intimidate you. I'm just stupid. I don't know why I thought he wouldn't do that. Mostly, I just thought he didn't care enough about anyone to bother. I told him I don't ever want to see his face again." Wren took a breath, trying to calm his racing heart. "He'll probably try to destroy me now."

Haven kissed him again. It was slow and sweet. He lingered over Wren's lips. When he pulled away, Haven looked like he felt all the same things Wren felt. "Don't worry about Dex. He came by here to apologize. In as much as Dex is capable of apologizing for anything. I don't think he realized I would react the way I did. Not that I'm over it. He hit in a spot that will probably always be vulnerable for me, but I really fucking love you and Finch. I just want to be with you two." Before Wren could admit all he wanted was the same thing, Haven took an audible breath and pushed on, sounding nervous as hell. "Also, I've been thinking, Finch is moving home soon. Who'll watch him while you work? You can't get just anyone. Maybe, even if you don't think you can ever be with me again, maybe I can stay with him."

Wren fought back another wave of tears. He really loved this man. Wren couldn't take another second of not saying it. "I'm in love with you. You know that, right? We are so lucky to have you." Wren believed that to his soul. There was no one else out there who was better for the job of taking on his little family. Wren came as part of a package deal and Haven hadn't seen that as a chore, or like he would take Finch too if he had no other choice. Haven wanted them both. Wren wasn't sure if he could ever forgive Dex for almost costing him this.

Haven dropped his head to Wren's chest and held on, as if trying to soak him in. Wren ran his fingers through his hair and sucked in his scent. "I say we wait until Finch wakes up and then see if he wants to stay with us tonight."

Haven lifted his head and met Wren's stare. "Us?"

Wren nodded. "Unless you have other plans."

"There's nowhere I would rather be."

He meant it. Wren could see it in his eyes. No one could possibly understand how much Wren needed Haven. Until Mister Haven crept into his heart, Wren hadn't realized how lonely and empty he felt, but Haven had seen inside him. Wren ran his fingers through Haven's hair again. No one would take this one from him. Wren would fight for him every bit as hard as he had fought for Finch. They were a family now.

IF WREN WAS THE LEAST BIT IMPATIENT TO BE alone with Haven, he didn't show it. He let Finch stay up as late as he wanted. Haven was fine with that. He wanted Finch good and asleep so he could have his way with Wren uninterrupted. Still, by the time they were finally alone, Haven was ready to scratch off his skin. He had spent the entire night before expecting he would never get to touch Wren again. Now he had hope and a second chance. He needed to taste Wren and know it was real. Wren had said he loved Haven. Haven wanted to hear it again and feel it in his bones.

Wren closed the bedroom door and glanced over his shoulder. "You should strip."

Despite his impatience, Haven couldn't stop himself from playing coy. "Why would I do that?"

A wicked smile stretched Wren's lips and Haven went hard. His mouth went dry. A fog settled in his brain. This was the version of Wren he had been incapable of resisting from the first moment they met. Wren took a step in his direction while stripping off his shirt. "Well, I'm about to be nude. I thought—maybe—you would like to be nude too, so we can compare notes, you know."

Something about Wren's mischievousness made Haven want to play. "What if I just want to cuddle?"

Wren unbuttoned his jeans and slid down his zipper, revealing his sexy cock. He was already hard for Haven. "We can cuddle all night as long as we do it with you inside me."

"Damn, you're beautiful." The words slipped out with no input from Haven's brain. Wren made him useless with his sexy body.

"Cock out, Haven. I want to sit on it."

Haven immediately sat on the edge of the bed and freed his erection. Wren finished undressing while eyeing Haven like his next meal. Haven couldn't stop himself. He stroked his cock while watching Wren's every move. Haven didn't think he as much as blinked. Wren headed for the bedside table and came out with lube. He held it up. "I'll probably need this. Don't you think?" As Haven looked on, Wren squeezed some onto his fingers. An evil-looking smile stretched his lips as he used the bed frame to prop up his foot. With his bottom lip held between his teeth, Wren lubed his asshole while Haven watched. Sweat broke out on Haven's skin. It was hot as hell watching Wren stroke his cock while pumping his own ass with two fingers.

"It could be you in here, if you took off your pants."

Haven scrambled out of his pants and into the middle of the bed. His dick stood proud and waiting.

Wren released a loud and put-upon-sounding sigh. "Maybe I'll do this instead." He dug around inside the drawer for a moment before coming out with a white plastic tube with a black button on the side. He slid the device over his dick and pressed the button. His head fell back, and his eyes closed. Wren's expression screamed ecstasy as the device sucked on his cock. Haven couldn't look away. Wren was mesmerizing. He knew exactly how to tempt men with his every move.

"Come sit on my dick while using that thing. I want to feel you come around my cock."

Wren didn't budge. Instead, he openly fucked his toy, teasing Haven.

Haven's voice hardened. It was out of his control. Wren could seduce anyone. Haven had unbending dominance on his side. "Wren."

Wren eyes snapped open. His lips parted on a pant as he caught sight of Haven. Haven knew how he looked. He was the Dom now. He felt it.

He fought the urge to growl as he spoke. "Sit on my dick. Now."

Wren carefully crawled onto the bed while making sure his toy stayed in place. He straddled Haven's body. Haven held his cock in place while Wren eased down on it. He fought the urge to close his eyes as Wren's tight heat slid down his erection.

"That's it, baby. Now fuck your toy while you ride me."

Wren lifted and thrust forward, doing exactly as Haven demanded while Haven watched. His abs stood out, showing off Wren's muscle control as he gave Haven exactly what he wanted. Wren's cheeks were flushed, and his lips were parted. With his eyes closed, Wren held tight to his toy as he thrust inside it. Haven fought the urge to move. He wanted Wren to control the pace. Haven loved it when Wren took what he wanted. Wren sucked in a ragged-sounding breath. His motions turned frantic. Haven couldn't look away. Starting at his toes, a pressure grew inside him as he watched Wren getting closer to the edge.

Wren's eyes opened. Their gazes met. Wren's body jerked and an orgasm punched Haven in the gut, knocking the air from him. He gasped as his body shook and his cock danced, pumping Wren's ass full of cum. Haven was on cloud nine, but he still wasn't satisfied. That one orgasm had been to take the edge off his hunger. The rest of the night would be about branding Wren with his love.

Haven shoved Wren's toy aside and rolled, pinning Wren beneath him. He stared down into the face of the man he loved more than his life and knew they would be okay. "By the time I'm done tonight, you'll call me Mister when we're in this bed."

Wren's mouth lifted in one corner into the sexiest smirk Haven had ever seen. "We'll see."

Yes, they would. After all, they had their entire lives left together for Haven to coax Wren into screaming that name. "Tell me you love me."

Wren's face softened. He cupped Haven's cheeks and held his stare. "I love you."

Haven couldn't doubt him. His heart melted. "I love you too." It was the last sweet gesture of the night.

TEN

LUNCH WITH DEX WAS NICE. Wren tried hard to be cold and not get sucked into their usual playful banter, but it wasn't easy. Haven and Dex were right. Dex was Wren's best friend. It had come as a surprise when—after a few months of Dex begging— Haven had suggested Wren give the guy a chance. Just not too much of a chance. But maybe the opportunity to be friends again. Wren had finally given in, and Dex hadn't made him sorry yet.

As Dex pulled into the driveway of the home that Wren now shared with Haven and Finch, Dex killed the engine. Wren's eyebrows rose. It wasn't like Dex to come inside his tiny place.

"What's up with you?"

Dex glanced his way and winked. "I'm keeping

my word to Haven to come in when I bring you home."

Wren froze with his hand on the door handle. "When did Haven say that?"

Dex winked. "When I called to ask his permission to take you to lunch. Let's go, fire sprite. He might not let me take you anywhere else if I break my word. God help me if I can only find people from Cubs for Rent to do things with me. That means I'll have to hire Colt and he fucking hates me."

"I would think that would make him twice as hot in your eyes."

A wicked-looking smile stretched Dex's lips. "It really does."

While shaking his head, Wren slipped from the car. His life was so different than he ever pictured it would be. Wren had no complaints. His step slowed as he caught sight of a note taped to the door. It was written in Finch's large and sloppy handwriting.

Finch's room is off limits. Secret meeting taking place.

Wren's forehead furrowed. "What are these boys up to now?" he muttered under his breath as he led Dex inside. Since Finch had moved home and Haven now took care of him full time while Wren worked, the pair had become inseparable. Haven had taught Finch more than he had learned with anyone else. He was a genius when it came to knowing exactly what Finch needed to thrive. That didn't mean Wren liked being left out. His curiosity was through the roof. Wren had been gone two hours. That meant Finch and Haven had been locked in Finch's bedroom for two full hours, working on this secret project. In the past few weeks, Wren had caught them whispering several times. They went quiet and tried looking innocent anytime Wren walked in the room. Now he was locked out of a bedroom in their home. His irritation rose. He wanted to play too.

Wren stamped down the hall and tried opening the door with Dex hot on his heels. It budged two inches before slamming in his face.

"We're not ready," Finch yelled, sounding panicked. Before Wren could completely snap, a giggle sounded through the door. "He almost saw." A smile stretched Wren's lips. He pressed his ear to the door, trying to hear their conversation. Finch was like a different child with Haven staying with him around the clock. It was like he was finally getting to be a kid.

"Stop pressing your ear to the door," Haven

yelled, making Wren jump away in guilt. "You can come in."

Wren turned the knob, still half expecting to get shut out. The door easily swung wide. His mouth fell open at the sight that met him. Finch was dressed in a white tux, matching Haven to the tiniest detail. His wheelchair had been decorated with golden cardboard cutouts, making him look like he drove a carriage.

"Oh my god. What is all this?"

While holding Finch's hand, Haven dropped to one knee. "We would like to request your permission to make this a real family."

A nervous-sounding chuckle escaped Wren. "What do you mean? I thought we were a family."

A sweet smile touched Haven's lips. "I would very much like to marry you and adopt Finch. This is my family, no matter what, but I want to make it official."

"Me too," Finch said, looking worried Wren might say no. "We made a buggy to sweep you away, in case you try to run."

Wren covered his mouth. He couldn't believe how much work they had put into this. Wren had to clear his throat to speak. He didn't know what he had done to deserve such an amazing man, but he would never take him for granted. "When is this big day happening?"

"Is that a yes?"

Wren nodded at Haven's question. "That's a yes."

"Then we had best get you dressed," Dex said, reminding Wren he still stood in the doorway at his back.

Wren glanced behind him. "What do you mean?"

Haven came to his feet, bringing Wren's gaze his way. He looked terrified he would get shot down. "Well, we were kind of hoping we could get started on our family today. Dex is friends with a judge who said he would sign a waiver so we could skip the waiting period. He's also agreed to perform the ceremony and Dex's lawyers have been working on putting together adoption papers for us. So, since everyone is here and—"

"Please," Finch said, interrupting. They both looked so hopeful, there was no way Wren could say no, especially since he didn't want to. Even though this was an adorable surprise, Wren wasn't caught off guard. They had talked about getting married several times and whispered behind closed doors about

Haven adopting Finch. It seemed Finch wasn't opposed.

Wren's arms rose and fell in a helpless gesture. There was no time like the present, he supposed. "I guess I better change."

Finch released a loud, ear-piercing screech as Haven closed the distance between them. Wren's heart skipped a beat at the happiness in Haven's eyes. This man was his. He was amazing, and by the end of the day, they would be married. Haven stole a kiss while Wren tried catching his breath. Wren and Haven turned as one to ensure Finch was included in their celebration. Wren held Haven's hand tightly in his as Finch rambled on in his excitement. He told Wren all about them decorating and building his carriage so they could have a fairytale wedding.

Finch gasped loudly, as if remembering something important. "Haven didn't give you your ring yet. He bought me one too. See," he said, holding out his hand to show off a gorgeous gold band. "He said he could never marry you unless he married me too, but not like I would be his husband. That's weird. I get to be his son or little brother, whichever I'm comfortable with. He's leaving it up to me. But he wrote vows for me too and they're really nice. I love you."

Wren blinked back tears as Finch spoke a mile a minute. In his heart, he knew there was no one else out there for them. Haven was right. No one could marry Wren without loving Finch too, but Haven went beyond all that. He made Finch a part of everything. There would never be anyone else for Wren. He had no doubts about his ability to spend the rest of his life with this wonderful person who had shown him the meaning of true and unselfish love. No one else could give him the happy life he knew Haven would provide. Not only for Wren, but for Finch as well. Life was perfect now.

Keep an eye out for the next Cubs for Rent, *Once He Breaks*.

Please consider leaving a review at the retailer where this book was purchased. Reviews really help with a book's visibility, which ensures I can continue writing. Thank you, Charity.

ABOUT THE AUTHOR

Charity Parkerson is an award winning and multi-published author with several companies. Born with no filter from her brain to her mouth, she decided to take this odd quirk and insert it in her characters.

*Eight-time Readers' Favorite Award Winner
    *2015 Passionate Plume Award Finalist
    *2013 Reviewers' Choice Award Winner
    *2012 ARRA Finalist for Favorite Paranormal Romance
    *Five-time winner of The Mistress of the Darkpath

Connect with her online:

--Join   my   street   team:
facebook.com/TeamCharityParkerson
    --Website: charityparkerson.com
    --Facebook:
facebook.com/authorCharityParkerson

facebook.com/TheMenofSin

--Twitter: twitter.com/CharityParkerso